THE
HARVEST
WAR

THE
HARVEST
WAR

MARTIN DAVIS

Columbus, Ohio

The Harvest War

Published by Gatekeeper Press
2167 Stringtown Rd, Suite 109
Columbus, OH 43123-2989
www.GatekeeperPress.com

ISBN (paperback): 9781642373578
eISBN: 9781642373561

Printed in the United States of America

PART ONE

THE PALE BLUE DOT

PROLOGUE

YEAR: 2109

The old man's fingers were gnarled, his nails cracked and yellow, and on the left hand where the pinky should be, there was only a tiny nub, a hint of a finger that once was. His scalp was spotted with age, mostly bald with wisps of brittle white hairs that grew away from his face and stuck out like porcupine quills. His face was etched with deep lines, crisscrossing together, a patchwork of wrinkles accented by several prominent scars.

He smoothed out his gray jacket and looked up at the younger man seated across the table from him. "How do I look?" he asked.

"Stunning," the younger man said. "But we're only recording your voice. It's just audio."

"Right, right," the old man said. "Well, it's a shame your audience is going to miss out on all this." He waved his hands up and down his body.

The younger man laughed. "Do you need anything before we start?"

The old man leaned back in his chair and looked up at the sky. They were sitting on a small patio overlooking a majestic garden, in what the old man recognized as the Japanese style, complete with a small bridge and tiny creek. He watched as water trickled around the bends of the fabricated pathway, landing in a pond filled with koi. He watched the fish swim, their vibrant colors forming a dizzying rainbow just beneath the water's surface.

He looked back at the younger man. "Sorry, what did you say?"

"I asked if you needed anything before we begin."

"Ah."

"What distracted you?"

"The water. Such a simple thing, but so beautiful to watch it flow. Especially considering how we almost lost it."

The younger man nodded.

"Well," the old man continued, "*lost* sounds like it was our fault. *Taken* would be a better term. But do I need anything? Do I need anything . . . I'll take some whiskey, if you have it."

"With ice?"

"Please."

The younger man's fingers danced over the table between them, and the old man saw glowing letters suddenly appear beneath his fingertips, then fade away as soon as contact was broken. The image of a glass appeared in lights on the table, and the younger man grazed his hand over it.

"How does that work?" the old man asked as he watched the last of the image disappear.

"The table?" the younger man said. "You've seen mech-tables before. They've been around for years."

The old man shook his head. "It all looks new to me. I don't understand it."

An insistent beeping sound suddenly rang through the air, and the younger man rose and crossed the patio to a small cabinet. He opened it and retrieved an already-poured glass of whiskey on the rocks, which he placed in front of the old man, who shook his head in disbelief.

"I swear," he muttered, and took a sip.

"Well," the younger man said. "Shall we begin?"

"If you like."

The younger man brushed his hand against the table again, and the old man saw three concentric circles appear for a moment before fading to nothingness. The younger man then sat back and crossed his legs.

"It's recording. Let's start from the beginning, shall we?"

"All right, then," the old man said, sipping his drink, "I guess you could say it started the way all good stories start. Lots of young, attractive, fit people having sex with each other."

The younger man laughed. "Really?"

"Oh, sorry, that's a different story I was thinking about. You want to hear about the Harvest War. Is that right?"

"That was the plan, yes."

"Right, then," the old man said. He smiled, revealing his crooked, yellowed teeth. "Well, *that* story begins much the way you've probably heard in school. All around the globe, people started seeing lights in the sky."

EIGHTY-EIGHT YEARS EARLIER . . .

CHAPTER 1

Kate shrieked with victory as she clutched the football to her chest. She had just caught a pass from thirty feet away, the longest throw she'd ever caught. "Alex! Did you see that?"

Alex Shephard looked up from the fire he was building. "I saw the whole thing, babe! You were amazing!"

She laughed. "Liar, you were building the fire!"

"I plead the fifth."

"Well, it was amazing. I'm totally getting drafted into the NFL next season."

He chuckled. A flame sprang up at the bottom of the wood pile he'd assembled, and he gently eased some dried brush underneath the growing blaze while delicately blowing on it. Soon enough, another stick of wood had ignited, and he sat back, pleased with himself.

It was a weekend leave, just a short respite from duty, but it was enough. He was excited when he called Kate and asked if she would be available to join him and his friends for a get-together on the beach, and overjoyed when she enthusiastically said she was. He looked

over at his buddies tossing the pigskin around with
Kate, sweating under the North Carolina summer sun.
Like him, they were all marines, all ranked lance corporal. They had gone through basic together, moving up
the ranks as a group, and Alex had grown to see Lenny
Hoffman, Mike Chan, and Natalia Vasquez as his family. Watching them bond with Kate was just about the
most beautiful damn sight he could imagine. It was the
first time they'd met his girlfriend of five years, and they
were the only ones on the planet who knew he was planning to propose to her once he saved up enough money
to buy a decent ring.

Hoffman, the least sporty of all of them, ditched
the game and trotted over to Alex. He grabbed two beers
from the nearby cooler and tossed one Alex's way. He sat
down on the sand and admired Alex's fire. "She's really
great, bro."

"Thanks. Once that top log catches, it'll be golden."

"Not the fire, moron," Hoffman said. "Kate."

Alex smiled. "Thanks, man. I think so, too."

"It's a good woman who'll stand by and wait for
grunts like us to get out."

"Speak for yourself. I'm going all the way up.
Sergeant major in no time."

Alex's face split into a comically wide grin, and
Hoffman burst out laughing. "Yeah, I'll believe that
when I see it."

Alex puffed out his chest. "Come on, look at these pecs. Look at 'em! This is a chest made to hold a ton of badges."

Hoffman kicked some sand at Alex, who shielded his face. "I've seen your pecs enough, thanks," Hoffman said, chugging his beer.

The sky was beginning to darken, and soon the others came to join them by the fire. Kate sat next to Alex, slid her arm into his, and leaned her head on his shoulder. "It's so awesome having you back," she said.

"It's just for the weekend, babe."

"I know, I know. Don't remind me."

Alex smoothed her long blond hair away from her face. Her hair hung down almost to her waist, and she was always threatening to cut it short. When she had met Vasquez earlier that day, Kate openly admired her buzz cut and told Alex maybe that was the route she'd go. He laughed then and told her she was free to do whatever she wanted, but he hoped to God she was kidding. He loved her hair. It made her look like a princess in a movie. *His* princess. As far removed from his life in the marines as possible, and he held that sacred. She was his safe space.

For hours, they sat around the fire, exchanging stories and jokes. The more beer they drank, the looser the lips of Alex's friends became. He found himself trying but failing to shut them down as they started to tell embarrassing stories about him, like the time he was found passed out in the latrine after an exhaustive day in basic, sitting on the toilet with his pants around his ankles. He worried she would wrinkle her nose, but Kate just laughed uproariously and squeezed him closer. The sky turned black and the stars slowly emerged around them as they talked. Alex thought for a moment that this was all he needed. Just these people, around this fire, on this beach. His best friends and the love of his life. What else could anyone possibly need?

"Check those out," Chan said. "That's weird."

His reverie broken, Alex followed Chan's pointed finger to two lights in the sky, moving in a parallel line. Aircraft. Flying very low.

"Private planes?" Vasquez suggested.

"Probably. Pretty tight formation, though," Alex said.

"Is that unusual?" Kate asked.

"Yeah," Hoffman said. "Unless—*whoa*!"

The lights took a sudden ninety-degree turn to the left and sped up so fast they became a blur. Then they were gone.

"Jesus freaking Christ!" Chan said.

As one, the marines stood, kicked sand into the fire, and packed up all their gear.

"What's going on?" Kate asked. Her voice was tight, strained. She was trying not to show she was afraid, Alex knew.

"Honestly? No idea," Alex said. "But we have to report that."

"Drones?" Chan said.

"I've never seen a drone that could move like that," Vasquez said.

"Most likely it's a friendly, possibly experimental," Alex said. "Don't want to take the chance, though. Let's head back in, grunts."

He took Kate by the shoulders and kissed her. "I'm so sorry to cut this short, babe. I'm going to drive you home and then I have to go back to base."

"Yeah, I got that part," Kate said. She mustered a smile. "Give me the rundown, though. One to ten, how freaked should I be?"

"Let's keep it at a 2.5 until we get more intel," he said.

She sighed. "Okay. I guess I can handle 2.5."

A humming sound suddenly drew everyone's attention skyward, and Kate gasped as they saw another pair of lights streak across the sky at an unimaginable speed.

That was the beginning.

* * *

For weeks, reports of strange lights in the sky came in from as far away as New Zealand and as close as the next county over. All over the world, in every country, people looked into the night sky and saw the impossible—lights moving at unfathomable speeds, zigzagging in a way no known technology could achieve. At first, every leader of every country accused every other leader of every other country of being the instigator of the lights, but as more time went by and no country claimed responsibility for the lights, what was really happening started to become evident.

We were being watched.

Word came down from the higher-ups that everyone was to be on call, ready to suit up at a moment's notice. Alex and his friends spent night after night in Camp Lejeune on edge, waiting for some new information, desperate for even an inkling of what was going on.

"You really think it's aliens?" Chan asked.

The four of them were sitting on their bunks, playing cards, while a radio played an endless stream of news at their feet.

"Don't see what else it could be," Alex said. "Any country would have taken credit for the tech by now, and no terrorist group could possibly have that much available to them. And even if they did, they wouldn't flaunt it. Doesn't make tactical sense."

"Still, man, *aliens*? I don't know," Hoffman said.

"What's that saying?" Vasquez said. "About how if you eliminate all the possibles, the impossible has to be true?"

"Once you eliminate the impossible," Alex quoted, "whatever remains, no matter how improbable, must be the truth."

"Spock said that, right?" Hoffman said.

Alex chuckled. "Pretty sure it was Sherlock Holmes."

"Maybe Spock quoted Sherlock Holmes?"

"That sounds plausible."

"So," Vasquez said, "if we've ruled out that a country or terrorist group is doing this, then . . ."

"Let's keep playing," Chan said, dealing the cards.

They played a few more rounds, each one pretending not to listen to the radio. But Alex was only half-concentrating on the game, as the subject of the next radio interview caught his ear.

"At first," the crisp radio newsman said, "most of the world's religious leaders condemned the ridiculous notion that there could be intelligent life outside of the earth. Nowhere in the Bible, the Torah, or the Quran was there ever mention of God creating life beyond the planet. But now it looks like that narrative might be shifting. We have with us today Archbishop Samuel Lennon, who has flown back to the United States following an emergency council that was called in the Vatican. Archbishop Lennon, welcome."

"Thank you, Scott, and just so we're clear, this was not an 'emergency' council. The Vatican has long dealt with the possibility and theological ramifications of life beyond our planet."

"I see. Thank you for clearing that up. Now, after days of deliberation, the official papal word on the subject was that if the lights are, in fact, indicative of extra-terrestrial life, then that would mean that these alien life forms come from a planet where its inhabitants are born without original sin. Is that correct, Archbishop?"

"That is correct, yes. According to our teachings, original sin occurred, of course, with Adam's rebellion in the Garden of Eden, which was obviously here on Earth. And therefore, if in fact the lights we've been seeing are extraterrestrial in nature, then the inhabitants of a distant planet would not know the stain of Adam's sin."

"So that means they wouldn't need to be baptized?"

"In order to enter the Kingdom of Heaven, no. Baptism serves to cleanse the soul of original sin and raise it up to be with Christ. For example, our holy mother Mary was the only human being born without original sin—"

"The Immaculate Conception."

"The Immaculate Conception, yes. That's right. Because she was born without this sin, there was no need to baptize her. The same would be true of beings from another planet. But they would still be embraced as brothers in Christ."

"But, Archbishop, let's be honest. There's no mention whatsoever of God creating life anywhere but here on Earth in any religious teaching—not the Old Testament, not the gospels. How would the existence of extraterrestrial life be compatible with the church's dogma?" the announcer asked.

"There are limits to man's imagination when it comes to his creative power," the Archbishop said, a bit sharply. "God has no such obstacle."

"Can we turn it off?" Hoffman whined. "I'm tired of hearing these guys talk. It's the same old shit. No one knows anything, but hey, let's talk about it twenty-four hours a day. 'Cause that'll help."

"Good call," Vasquez said. She reached down and hit the radio's off button. "I'm sick of it, too. I could use a beer, man."

"Ugh, same here," Chan said. "This waiting around is the worst. No beer, no leave. I just want some nachos, bro."

"Really, guys?" Hoffman said. "We're facing the end times and you're talking about beer and nachos?"

"Yeah, it's called priorities," Chan said.

"I'm gonna hit the head," Alex said. He threw his cards down on the table and walked off. As he exited the room, he heard Vasquez whisper, "What bit his ass?"

Alex went to the bathroom and was relieved to find it empty. No doubt, across the entire base, marines were huddled around radios or watching the news on televisions and computers, anxious to hear more about the lights in the sky, nervous about what the answers might be. But Alex, who had been a devout Christian his whole life, found he couldn't even begin to contemplate what the presence of extraterrestrial life might mean. *If there really are aliens behind those lights*, he wondered, *what if . . .*

. . . what if they were made by something other than God?

"Shephard, are you in here?" a voice called from outside.

Chan, Alex thought.

He ran the cold water and splashed some on his face as Chan came in. "Hey, man, you're going to want to come with me. Right now. We got to see this."

"See what?" Alex asked, grabbing a few paper towels and wiping his face.

"The aircraft those lights belong to? They started *landing*."

Alex felt all the blood rush out of his face. Numbly, he followed Chan to the rec room, where dozens upon dozens of marines had gathered around the enormous television, watching a live feed from CNN. The station was airing footage that had just been taken a few minutes earlier, of a diamond-shaped craft slowly lowering itself to the earth. It was sleek, with no apparent windows to the inside, and made of what looked like a turquoise-tinted metallic substance.

"This is like something out of a goddamn movie," Vasquez whispered, shaking her head.

"This just can't be real," another grunt said. "It can't. There's no way." There were a few murmurs of agreement.

The voice of a female news anchor spoke over the footage. "Again, this is what happened just a few moments ago, and we're getting reports that these ships have been landing in many countries all over the planet. This particular footage is in the mountains in the remote town of Wyalusing, Pennsylvania, and is being covered by a local news crew there. We're now going to switch to an in-house crew that's covering the landing of another ship in Tallahassee. Rick, can you hear us?"

The television feed switched to another shot of an identical ship in what looked like a park. A middle-aged man, his face taut and nervous, kept looking back and forth from the ship to the camera.

"Hi, Sandra, yes, I can hear you, and so far there's been no change as the ship continues to lie in what appears to be a . . . well, a relatively dormant state . . ."

"So, what, they're just waiting in the car?" Vasquez said. "Jesus, show your faces, man!"

"Seriously," Hoffman said.

"Shhh!" another marine hissed.

The reporter on the screen wiped at the sweat on his brow. "As we said, this craft landed approximately five minutes ago, and it would seem that's the case basically the world over, or at least that's our understanding at this moment."

A coordinated plan, Alex thought. He forced himself to swallow.

"But as we've said, Diane, so far there's been no— *oh, my God!* Oh, my God."

There were gasps around the room as everyone watched what was unmistakable on the television screen. A rectangle of light appeared on the outside of the craft.

A door.

"Scott?" the female anchor's voice sounded. "Are we seeing this correctly?"

"Yes, Diane, what—good lord—what looks like a door has appeared on the side of the—oh, sweet Jesus. This is happening. This is happening . . .This may very well be mankind's first contact with an extraterrestrial species . . ."

Before the astonished eyes of the marines, the metal rectangle dissolved, as though it had been nothing more than vapor. In its place stood one solitary figure, barely visible in the dim lighting. Human in shape, it stood at a giant height, seven feet tall at least, with no visible hair on its head.

But of course, the most immediately noticeable attribute to its silhouette were the enormous wings that sprouted from its back.

2109

"Wings?" the younger man said. His brow was furrowed, confused.

The old man took a sip of his whiskey. "They weren't really wings, of course. Nothing even solid back there. When the Seraphim arrived, the first ones to make contact were wearing their – what do you call it – those things on their back, the jet whatever . . ."

"The energy propulsion systems. Or jet packs, people call them sometimes."

"Right, the jet pack. Apparently something about the way the light catches the gas that comes out of them, it makes it look like glowing wings. But you can imagine how everyone reacted. Come on—a giant humanoid creature with wings drops out of the sky? Immediately everyone had the same thought."

"Angels."

The old man nodded and took another sip. "It's what people thought when they first started showing up thousands of years ago, and it's what people first thought at the Revelation of 2021. And in a way, they were right, I suppose."

The younger man laughed, but there was no humor in it. "The Seraphim were hardly angels."

"Well, of course not, but that's where the idea of angels came from."

"Can you specify?" the younger man said. He pointed to the mech-table's recording light. "For posterity."

The old man leaned forward. "Before the Revelation of 2021, we thought humankind came up with the idea of angels. Well, I guess the more religious folk thought they were real and always with us, but the point is no one suspected the truth: that the Seraphim had been visiting the earth since way before the idea of a written language was even a glimmer in a cave-painter's eye.

"They were there at the beginning, watching the human race grow and evolve. Every ancient and inexplicable wonder you can think of is due to them. The pyramids, Stonehenge, the Nazca landing strips, even those, what were those things . . . the heads . . ."

"The heads?" the younger man asked.

"I'm getting old and my memory's going. The crystal head things?"

"Oh, the Crystal Skulls."

"There it is. Every feat that seemed impossible for early man to achieve, it was because of the guidance of the Seraphim. Secretly, of course. But the Seraphim weren't perfect. They slipped up sometimes, people saw them. And so whispers of magical creatures from the sky began. And they became, in our eyes, angels."

"How did we learn what they call themselves? I mean, *seraphim* is of course a Hebrew word that means archangel. I can't imagine that's a coincidence."

"No, of course not. I think the most likely scenario is one where the early Semites had some sort of relationship or meeting with one of them, and learned the name of their species."

The younger man leaned forward. "And what about the blood—"

"I think we're getting ahead of ourselves," the old man said. "My brain's addled enough as it is. If I don't tell the story in chronological order I don't know if I'll be able to give you everything you need."

"Of course, sorry about that," the younger man said. He leaned back. "So the Seraphim landed. What happened next?"

"Well, that would be the greatest horror ever visited upon the human race. They started taking human beings as prisoners, throwing them into detainment camps. No one knew why at the time. The militaries of the world couldn't work together to create any sort of unified front, so people were helpless, just absolute lambs to the slaughter. One day the world was normal, and a couple of weeks later, it was a nightmare. Hell on earth. People running from abandoned house to abandoned house, trying to find shelter, trying to evade the squadrons of Seraphim patrolling the streets looking to grab humans and haul them into their camps. And all the Seraphim would tell humanity was to lie down and take it."

"They spoke our languages?"

"Apparently," the old man said, "they invented our languages."

CHAPTER 2

"**I**ncoming, three o'clock!" Hoffman shouted.

Alex whipped around and aimed his M16 assault rifle at the approaching Seraphim. There were three of them flying, moving fast on the jet stream of their packs, the ghost of wings behind them turning Alex's stomach. They evaded his fire with ease, and Alex gritted his teeth.

The bastards were just so damn *fast*.

They flew about four feet above the road, darting and swerving to avoid his gunfire. The most terrifying thing about them, Alex thought, was that, despite soaring at fifty miles per hour, they were silent. Their jet packs produced no noise, and they didn't yell or scream. They didn't even talk to each other to communicate. They just moved, silent and merciless.

Alex let loose another spray of bullets, moving the rifle in an erratic pattern. This did the trick—he clipped one of the Seraphim on the shoulder, and it rolled over in the air and crashed into an abandoned car. The other two fell back.

"Get the lead out, Hoffman!" Alex yelled. Hoffman gunned the engine and whipped the car around a corner, causing Alex to fall back against the seat.

"Nice," he said.

"Hey, you asked for it," Hoffman said. "Are they still on our tail?"

Alex looked behind them. The Seraphim were no longer in pursuit. "That's a negative on the bogeys."

"At last, good news. I really wasn't looking forward to getting touched by an angel any time soon."

Alex looked out at the buildings flashing by. He and Hoffman had driven into Jacksonville in search of food and supplies. The run was fairly successful, as they had discovered a drug store that had yet to be looted. They loaded the jeep up with armloads of precious medical equipment. Suddenly, Hoffman got a bad feeling and turned the ignition. It was then that Alex spotted the roving Seraphim and knew his friend was right—it was time to go.

It was the closest they'd come yet to being captured. He didn't want to risk that again.

Four weeks had passed since the Seraphim made themselves known, and in that time the world had gone to hell, and fast. Alex remembered something his old drill sergeant had said on his very first day of basic: "In war, life doesn't change gradually—it flips on a dime before you can say 'puke.' You have to be ready."

There was no way to be ready. Not for something like this. War had fallen on them from the heavens above in a coup unprecedented in the whole of human history. But he and his fellow grunts were doing the best they could, trying to preserve what was left of the human race.

They arrived back at Camp Lejeune without further incident. Alex called out to the men who acted as guards, standing atop the hastily fortified gate. They waved to him and opened the gate. Hoffman sped in and Alex listened to the gate hastily being shut behind them. Alex knew a gate was only so much protection against enemies that could fly, but fortunately he had discovered that their "wings" were mechanical in nature and could be taken out with a direct shot. Fry the wings, and the bastards were just as glued to the ground as mankind. There had been an attack on the base the day after the Seraphim had landed, but they weren't expecting such an elegant response from the marines inside, and all had been quiet since then.

But Alex knew it was just a matter of time.

Once the goods they'd brought with them were handed out, Alex raced back to the barracks, which had been converted into living quarters for anyone lucky enough to make it to the camp without being picked up by the Seraphim's rovers. Now that he was reasonably safe again, there was someone he wanted to see.

He entered the barracks and saw Chan easing his broken arm into a sling. He'd been injured in the first attack and had been working his ass off to rehabilitate as quickly as he could. Alex knew the feeling. Nothing was worse than thinking you were a burden to everyone else. That's not the way a Marine is built.

Alex trotted over to him. "Hey, Chan, how you doing?"

"Better, man, thanks."

"You seen Kate?"

Chan nodded in the direction of the doors across the way. "Infirmary."

"Thanks, buddy. Hang tight."

Chan grumbled a response, and Alex headed through the doors and into another area of the barracks that had been converted into a makeshift infirmary. He saw Kate wrapping gauze around an old woman's ankle. The woman whimpered.

"I'm so sorry we don't have anything for the pain," Kate said, continuing the delicate process. She turned and saw Alex, and relief crossed her face. "Alex!"

He came to her side. "We raided a drug store. Lots of medication. Definitely pain relief."

The old woman let out a relieved sigh.

"Darren!" Kate called to a young boy nearby. "Can you go to the supply room and pick up something for Mrs. Weiss?"

"Sure thing!" the boy, no more than fifteen, called back, and took off out of the room at record speed.

"He'll be back in no time, Mrs. Weiss," Kate said.

"Oh, thank you, dear," the old woman said, leaning her head back on the cot.

"Do you need anything else before I go?"

"You've been an angel, sweetheart," Mrs. Weiss said, gripping Kate's arm. "God bless your good nature."

Kate smiled, then took off her latex gloves and moved away with Alex. Once they were out of sight of the old woman, she embraced and kissed him. "Thank God you're back. I was terrified."

"Me, too. But I had Hoffman with me."

"I know. But still . . ."

"How's everything going here?"

Kate frowned. "I kind of wish I had more than one year of medical school under my belt before the apocalypse happened. I'm in way over my head here."

"I know, baby. But after Doc bit it in the first attack, you're the most qualified person here. That makes you our chief medical officer."

Kate let out a frustrated groan. "Fantastic."

Alex looked at her as she rubbed her eyes with one hand. Even at her most distressed, she was the most beautiful thing he had ever seen. He remembered his plan, his wonderful, crazy plan of asking her to marry him, once he had saved up enough to buy a damn ring. Before death and destruction had rained down on them from above. Had it really just been four weeks?

"Alex, listen," Kate said. "There's something I have to tell you."

"What is it, babe?"

As she opened her mouth to speak, the far wall exploded into dust. Alex instinctively grabbed Kate and pulled her down to the ground, covering her body with his own. All around them, people began screaming and running out of the infirmary.

"Are you okay?" Alex shouted.

Kate nodded, grimacing, her eyes wide with terror.

"Come on," Alex said, and pulled her up. He started toward the exit, but as he did, she pulled back on his wrist. "Wait! Mrs. Weiss!" she said, and sprinted back into the infirmary.

"Kate!" Alex yelled, and followed her in.

Dust was everywhere, clouding his vision, but he was just able to make out the shape of Kate kneeling over a lump on the floor. He ran over to her and looked down at what was beneath her. Mrs. Weiss. Or what was left of her.

He looked up at Kate, who was sobbing. He heard himself speaking as though listening to someone else. Heard the words, but barely realized it was him saying them. "Come on, baby. She's dead. We have to go. We have to go."

Numb, he grabbed Kate's wrist and ushered her out of the room as another explosion demolished the wall to their left. They both hunched over and sped up.

"What do we do?" Kate asked.

"We've got to get to Command!" Alex shouted, hurrying her along.

He heard the sound of gunfire and risked a look behind him. Seraphim were pouring in through the newly made holes in the walls and being met with gunfire. He saw someone raising hell at them with an assault rifle. From the shaved head and small frame, he recognized the person as Vasquez. He wanted to go back and give her an assist, but he had to get Kate to the interior of the base, away from the fighting.

Keep her safe, Alex, he told himself. *Keep her safe at all costs.*

Together, they ran through the chaos, choking on dust and ash as it filled their mouths, ducking instinctively when they heard the sound of gunfire or the hideous *vroom* of the Seraphim's weapons. They pushed ever onward, until Alex practically tripped over someone on the floor. He looked down, saw it was Hoffman with a laceration on his head, with blood pouring from it.

"Hoff!" he said, then reached down and shook his friend. Hoffman's eyes were closed, but they fluttered open and he locked eyes with Alex.

"Shit," Hoffman whispered. "They're in. They're fucking *in!*"

"Come on!" Alex said. He and Kate helped Hoffman to his feet, and the three of them kept moving. Eventually they wove through the destruction and made their way out of the barracks.

Though he tried to keep his head down and keep moving forward, Alex couldn't help but look up at the sky as they ran. "Oh, my God," he whispered.

The sky was full of Seraphim. Angels of death. *This can't be real,* he thought. *This is something out of goddamn Revelation.*

They raced across the open field toward the Base Theater, which had been designated as Command Central after the original building was destroyed in the first attack. Alex looked up again. So far it looked as though the escapees hadn't been spotted, or if they had, they weren't considered a perceivable threat. They kept running. One hundred yards left.

Seventy-five.

Fifty.

Thirty.

Almost there, Alex thought.

But then an enormous shape, so fast it was a blur, fell in front of them. The Seraphim crouched a bit when it landed. But then it straightened its legs, rising to its full height of seven and a half feet tall. Its face would have been beautiful were it not for the pure white eyes, which showed no pupil or iris, and the sheen of metal that dotted its face. Some scientists had postulated that the Seraphim utilized a sort of biomechanical inter-face—they were part machine. Now that Alex was seeing one for the first time up close, he realized he couldn't possibly care less what the metal on their skin meant. He and Kate and Hoffman were exposed, and he had no weapon.

The Seraphim took a step toward them and raised one hand, which started to glow. Alex knew what was coming—a laser would propel forth from that hand, rendering them all unconscious. He'd seen footage of it a dozen times already. After that, they would be collected and taken God knows where.

He held Kate close and stared at the Seraphim, preparing himself—when its head burst apart to the chorus of a machine gun. Blood and chunks of skull and brain sprayed up and back in a hideous fountain. "Die, fucker!" a woman's voice came from behind them.

They whipped around and saw Vasquez hobbling along, the gun tucked underneath one arm, Chan leaning on the other shoulder. There was a nasty wound on her right thigh, and the pant leg beneath it was stained dark all the way to her boot. Chan didn't look any better.

Vasquez pushed past Alex and let loose another spray of bullets into the dead Seraphim's abdomen.

Alex looked up and saw two more coming their way.

"Move! Get inside!" he screamed, and the five of them sprinted the remaining distance toward the Base Theater. Someone was at the door, and they opened it in time for the five of them to make it through. Alex saw the person behind the door was Corporal Peters, who had been a stoic, quiet man before the attack. Now he pointed frantically for them to keep moving, his eyes wild. As they entered, he slammed the door closed and began fortifying it.

There was the sound of an explosion outside, and they all turned and saw the barracks they had just been inside not four minutes earlier erupt in flames, as explosions went off inside. And right outside the door, a

Seraphim had landed. It crouched down and locked eyes through the window with Corporal Peters.

Peters whipped around to Alex and the rest. "Get to the auditorium, Marines!" he shouted. He bent down and scooped up the M16 lying at his feet as the Seraphim watched him, eerily silent.

Never having needed to hear orders twice, Alex wrangled everyone in the direction of the auditorium. He shouldered one of the doors open, and they all rushed in. Inside it was dark, but when his eyes adjusted to the dim light, he saw Master Sergeant Brady standing near the stage, looking over papers on a fold-out table. Brady was a large man, stern of face, bald, with a severe mustache covering his upper lip. Alex had always been intimidated by the man when he saw him around the base. Now he just seemed tired, resigned.

Brady looked up as the five of them entered, then motioned for them to come closer. "Double time, Marines!" he barked, staring at the papers.

Alex and the others quickened their pace and soon stood at the table, looking down at the papers on it. They were mostly maps, with a few other documents scattered around. "The camp's fallen," Brady said without preamble, grabbing all the papers and stacking them together. "Did anyone else get inside with you?"

Alex swallowed. "It was just the five of us, sir."

Brady looked over at them for the first time. "Three of you are injured?" He looked at Kate. "And you're not a marine."

"I'm a medical student," Kate said.

"Wonderful," Brady muttered. He stuffed the papers into a folder and tied it shut. He handed the packet to Alex. "Four weeks ago this was Eyes Only, but considering the world's gone to shit, Uncle Sam thought it best to send out this intel to any functioning facility with access to manpower and weaponry, which means us. In the event of occupation, we were to send out whoever we could, which means you. So now I'm authorizing each of you to view this material."

"What is it, sir?" Alex asked.

"Information that might be of some value to the preservation of the human race. In brief, Uncle Sam's highest-ups knew about the Seraphim before they showed up last month—"

"What!" Kate asked.

Brady breezed right over her. "But for obvious reasons they kept it black. This folder contains the whereabouts of three Special Forces agents. They're sleepers, off the grid. Put into forced hiding by the government to await orders. We were prepping a black ops contingent to activate them. They were supposed to leave tomorrow. But seeing as how that's no longer a possibility, this mission is up to the five of you."

"You're not coming, sir?" Alex asked.

Brady moved from behind the table and displayed a makeshift tourniquet he had wrapped around his leg. "I'd only slow you down, son. Even more than the injured you currently have. Besides, you'll need someone to cover your escape."

"You think the Seraphim knew about the black ops mission, sir?" Chan asked. "That's why they attacked?"

Brady looked over at him. "Son, at this point I wouldn't be surprised if those fuckers were goddamn psychic. Anyhow, the sleeper agents each have intel about the Seraphim that we don't, but each one of them only knows a third of the whole story, or at least the whole story as we understand it. So you'll need to find all three. From there, I don't know what happens next. I wish I did."

"Wait," Kate said. "Sorry, how do we know these agent guys are still where the maps say they are? Wouldn't they have come out of hiding when the Seraphim landed?"

"Their orders were clear. No movement until activation, even in the event of a global catastrophe. And Special Forces follow their orders."

Kate said, "But we can't just *call* them?"

"These men are unreachable by any technological means. That's sort of the whole point of 'off the grid,' ma'am."

"One problem, sir," Vasquez said. "We're trapped in here."

"Not exactly. Behind the stage is a trapdoor that leads to a tunnel. Take this."

The master sergeant removed a hand grenade from a bag on the table and handed it to Alex. Alex saw Kate's eyes widen when she saw the weapon. As a civilian, the most weaponry she had been exposed to before the Seraphim invasion was his sidearm. Now she was getting a close-up view of all the toys of war.

"After you're inside, take down the beams supporting the ceiling behind you. Collapse them so no one can follow you."

Alex took the grenade and nodded. "Understood, sir."

"The tunnel leads out of the camp and underneath the riverbed. It opens on the other side, out onto the field by Rhodes Point Road. Once you're out, acquire the first vehicle you can and get the hell out of here."

"Yes, sir."

A sharp scream sounded from outside the doors, and they could make out the sound of the Seraphim's weapons. Alex knew the scream belonged to Corporal Peters. The Seraphim had breached their defenses.

"Get out of here, now!" Brady hissed at them.

The five of them dashed toward the back of the stage and found the trapdoor. Alex opened it and ushered everyone in before him. Once they were all through, he turned quickly toward Brady. The last thing he saw before dropping into the tunnel was the master sergeant facing the doors and lifting his M2HB machine gun in preparation for what was about to come.

Then Alex jumped down, and there was nothing but darkness.

CHAPTER 3

"**G**o! Go! Go!" Alex yelled to Kate and the rest.

Once they were safely out of range, he shouted, "Fire in the hole!" He bit down on the safety pin ring, yanked it out, and tossed the grenade at the beams nearest the entrance. Then he took off as fast as his legs would move. He could feel the blood pumping wildly through his veins, the rapid pulsing against his carotid artery. He knew his body was actively going through the fight-or-flight adrenaline rush, and as he ran, it occurred to him they might have to change that particular turn of phrase when dealing with enemies who were capable of literal flight.

The strangest things pop into your head when you might be about to die, Alex thought.

He heard the explosion behind him, followed by the rush of dirt and rock and splintered wood crashing down together, forming what he hoped was an impenetrable barrier. The Seraphim might be technologically superior, but they were still physical creatures bound by the laws of physics, and as far as Alex knew, they couldn't pass through solid matter. He just prayed he and his friends had enough time to escape.

After twenty minutes, they reached the end of the tunnel. It led up to a circular cover, flat against the ground, no doubt meant to look like a sewer entrance. Alex pushed the cover back, poked his head out and looked up at the sky. It was, he was grateful to find, filled only with stars. The Seraphim were still concentrating all their energy on Camp Lejeune. It hadn't even occurred to them to look past the river.

"Let's move!" Alex said. Kate jumped out behind him and lowered her hand to Vasquez as Alex reached down to help Hoffman up. Once they were out, Alex and Vasquez pulled Chan out, and they were on the move once again. The tunnel put them out on an open field, way more exposed than Alex would have liked.

"We've got to find cover and a vehicle," he said.

"Get me to a set of wheels and I can hot-wire it," Hoffman wheezed, "but the trick is actually, you know . . . getting me there."

He staggered and fell to one knee. Kate stooped down next to him.

"Shit. Lenny? Hey, Lenny, look at me," she said. She snapped her fingers in front of his face a few times. His eyes had become glazed, but on her authoritative tone, they snapped back into focus.

"Yes, ma'am," he said.

"Lenny, you probably have a concussion, given the injury to your head. You're probably feeling a little tired right now—"

"Yeah, I am."

"So it's really, really important that you stay awake. Okay? You got it?"

Hoffman nodded, widening his eyes a few times to revive himself.

"Do you think you can walk?"

He nodded again, and with the help of Chan and Vasquez, got back to his feet.

They moved away from the river, away from the base, and the swarm of Seraphim flying above it. They found the road with its merciful cover of trees on either side, and Alex let himself relax just a bit. There were large houses spread out along one side of the road. A few of them even had vehicles in front of them. No doubt when the families who had occupied those houses took their leave for the promised safety of military bases, they departed in one vehicle and abandoned any others they might own. That was typical civilian behavior, Alex knew. Stay together at all costs. It made much more tactical sense to take every vehicle you could in case there were mechanical failures, but that's not how nonmilitary thought. They chose the perceived safety of numbers over the more realistic safety of contingency plans.

Of course, Alex thought, the irony was that he and his friends were about to do just that. What mattered the most, what might make the difference between life and death, was speed. They needed to put as much distance between them and the camp as possible.

They stopped at the first vehicle they came to—a midsize Chevrolet SUV. Big enough for all five of them. It would have to do. And fortunately, it wasn't even locked.

"Do your magic, Hoff," Alex said.

Hoffman opened the driver's side door and shuffled in. He pulled out his utility knife and began prying the panels off the ignition cylinder. As he worked, Kate walked over to Chan and Vasquez.

"How are you guys holding up?" she asked.

"My leg's pretty bad," Vasquez winced.

"I'm okay," Chan said. "Arm's still busted but other than that, just a few cuts and bruises."

"Alex, let me see your knife," Kate said. Alex handed it to her. "Can you look in the back of the car and see if there's anything I might be able to use to bind up these wounds?"

Alex opened the trunk and peered inside. There wasn't much: a jack, a tire iron, a roll of duct tape, and a few old newspapers. Not exactly the jackpot. He listed the items for Kate, and she responded, "Okay, bring the tape."

He came back around the car to discover that Kate had cut open part of Vasquez's pant leg, revealing a nasty, jagged wound on her thigh. To his surprise, Kate ripped off a piece of duct tape, pulled Vasquez's skin as close together as she could, and slapped the tape right over the wound. Vasquez howled in pain, then bit down hard on her lip.

"Sorry about the pain, girl," Kate said.

"Eh, it builds character," Vasquez panted. Beads of sweat appeared on her forehead.

"This should get stitches, but this is the best we can do for now. And hey, scars are sexy, right?"

"Damn straight."

The sound of an engine turning over filled the air. "Got it!" Hoffman said triumphantly.

"Great," Alex said. "Move over. I'm driving."

"But I'm the vehicle guy," Hoffman objected.

"You're also the concussed guy. I'm the only uninjured marine here, so I drive," Alex said. "Move over, bud."

Hoffman frowned but ceded the seat, shifting over into the passenger side. Alex was grateful when he looked at the gas gauge and found it almost full. A few minutes later, they were on the road, speeding past dark streets and eerily empty houses. Hoffman and Vasquez kept a lookout on the sky as Kate and Chan poured over the documents Master Sergeant Brady had given Alex. Alex pressed down hard on the accelerator. Why the hell not? There were no cops to give them speeding tickets and no other cars to collide with.

Alex bit his lip when he thought of the camp. All those people. So many of them civilians. All dead, or captured, only to be thrown into the detainment camps, subjected to God knows what. He looked up at the sky for a moment, took in the endless expanse of stars. As a child, he had always looked up at the night sky, but he'd never envisioned aliens beyond the scope of his sight.

It had always been heaven.

As he got older, he knew that heaven was most likely not physically located in the sky. But it still brought him comfort to think about. All the souls of the world who'd passed on, looking down on them. Smiling, worrying, but most importantly, *being there.*

He absentmindedly brought his hand to his shirt, felt the hard metal underneath it—the tiny cross on a chain he always wore. While he'd always been a strict man of faith, he'd never put too much stock in *blind* faith. His belief in God didn't come from nowhere. He'd heard all the arguments on all sides, and he'd given them years of serious contemplation. And for a long time now, he was secure in the conclusion that everything happened as designed by God's hand. He knew that some people found evolution to be sufficient proof for the randomness of the universe, but to him it seemed so clear that such an incredible, fascinating process was surely guided by a higher power. Every stage of evolution was an utter miracle. How could it be proof of anything else *but* the existence of God?

But now . . . now he wasn't so sure. He thought of the Seraphim that had landed by them, the one that Vasquez killed. That was the closest he'd ever physically been to one of them. The thing's face haunted him. Its white eyes and metallic glisten were the most alien thing he could imagine, but the design of its face—eyes, nose, mouth, ears, all where they were supposed to be—was so distinctly human it made him shudder.

He remembered touring a military robotics facility once where they were working on androids. They were the most lifelike robots Alex had ever seen, and bizarrely, this made him feel sick. When he mentioned this to one of the robotics engineers, the man told him of "the uncanny valley." It was a turn of phrase used to describe feelings of revulsion when confronted with something almost, but not quite, human.

Alex remembered the Seraphim's face and grimaced. He didn't imagine that particular valley could possibly get more uncanny.

* * *

They drove for days. After the first night, Kate took over driving, letting Alex get some sleep. He woke when they stopped suddenly. Immediately he sat up, alert and ready.

"What's happening?" he asked.

"Kate stopped. She said she felt sick," Chan said, rubbing his bleary eyes.

Alex opened the door and got out of the car. "Kate?" he asked. "Babe, you okay?"

She had run over to the bank of grass on the side of the road, and from the sound of it was vomiting profusely. "I'm okay," she said between heaves. "I'm fine, really. Probably just a little aftereffect from, you know, that whole almost dying thing."

"You don't need to be a champ, baby," Alex said. "If you're sick—"

"I'm fine." She wiped her mouth and stood up. "Never been better. See?"She gave him a wide smile, then doubled over and vomited some more.

After she recovered a bit, they got back in the car and continued driving west. The maps indicated that the first sleeper cell agent was located in Kisatchie National Forest in Louisiana, and so that was their destination.

"The Kisatchie Hills, within the national forest, are protected as a national wilderness area," Chan read. "That's where our guy is."

"Does it say anything about him? Any identifying information?" Alex asked.

"Just that his name is Kevin Hartinger and he's forty-seven years old," Chan answered. "Beyond that, not much. Former CIA. Went to Special Forces, as it seemed like the best place for a man of his skills, which are apparently Liam Neeson-esque in scope."

The others chuckled.

"How long has he been Green Beret?" Vasquez asked.

Chan looked over the paperwork. "Twenty years."

This was met with a chorus of whistles from the marines. "Damn," Hoffman said. "This guy's no joke."

"Well," Alex said, "considering Uncle Sam entrusted him with the knowledge that we're not alone in the universe and a third of the intel about what to do about it in case our neighbors ever come knockin', I'm not too surprised."

"Point," Hoffman said.

They stopped just a mile outside the national forest and took refuge for the night in an abandoned farm house. It was a modest, two-story affair, and Alex was grateful to find it had three working bathrooms with running water. What's more, there was a linen closet stocked with clean towels. This meant one extremely precious thing.

Showers.

It's amazing the things you take for granted until they're taken away from you, Alex thought.

After they were both clean, Alex and Kate headed to the master bedroom. The others insisted they take it, as it was the only room with a double bed.

"And I'm sure as hell not sleeping in the same bed as one of these two pervs," Vasquez said.

"You wish!" Chan and Hoffman replied in unison.

Alex chuckled. Some things never changed. Even when everything in the world around you does.

Alex sat on the bed and held Kate's hand. "You feeling better, babe?" he asked.

Kate took a deep breath and let it out in a heavy sigh. "Well, the nausea's alleviated," she said. "But we need to talk about something."

"What is it?"

"Last month I missed my period. That isn't a big deal – it happens to me sometimes. But that coupled with the throwing up . . ." She trailed off. "I think you know where I'm going with this."

Alex felt like there was a golf ball stuck in his throat. "Are you sure?"

"I was due for the next period four days ago, so yeah, I'm pretty sure."

Alex sat back against the headboard and tried to breathe.

"So . . . what do you think?" Kate asked.

"I . . ." Alex said. "I . . ."

"Yeah," Kate said. She smiled humorlessly. "Same."

Alex looked around. "How did this happen?"

She laughed. "Well, human biology doesn't change just because aliens show up. You do certain things and you're still gonna get the same results."

He nodded and rubbed his eyes. "We'll get through this, babe. We'll find these sleeper guys and let them take it from there."

"Alex, the whole world's gone to hell in, what, four weeks? What makes us think it'll ever go back to the way it was?"

"It won't. But I think humanity has proven it's pretty scrappy. This'll be over some day. And hey, who knows what kind of master intel the sleepers have? They might already know how to beat them."

"I hope you're right," Kate said. She lay her head down on the pillow. "I'm afraid to go to sleep. But I'm so damn tired."

"Then close your eyes, baby," Alex said. He kissed her and watched as her eyes fluttered closed. In no time, she was out cold.

Alex looked around the room. Before the invasion, news of a baby would have made him happier than anything in the world. But now . . .

"Shit," he said to the walls.

* * *

The next morning, Alex led the way as they approached a tiny shack in the woods.

"Kevin Hartinger!" he called out. "My name is Alex Shephard. I'm a lance corporal in the United States Marines. I'm here with my fellow officers. We were at Camp Lejeune when it fell to a Seraphim attack. Master Sergeant Will Brady gave us your intel. We're here to collect you on behalf of the U.S. government. Consider yourself activated."

He scratched his head, then added, "Uh . . . *sir.*"

All five of them looked around expectantly. Nothing.

"Maybe he's not here anymore," Kate said. "The master sergeant seemed convinced, but, I mean, what with the end of the world and all . . ."

"He's here," Vasquez said. "Somewhere. Green Berets follow orders, even if it means their death. They don't punk out no matter what."

Alex looked at the shack. It seemed unoccupied, but looks could be deceiving. Especially when sleeper agents were involved. "I'm going in," he said.

"You sure?" Chan asked. "He might have gone a little nuts with all the seclusion. This could be dangerous."

"Dangerous is pretty relative these days," Alex said. "And we don't exactly have the luxury of time."

He squared his shoulders and walked toward the house. Just as he was almost at the door, he heard Hoffman yell out behind him, "Shephard, *wait!*"

But it was too late. Alex put his foot down in front of him, and one second later he was hanging upside down three feet above the ground, swinging wildly back and forth. He looked up and saw his ankle was caught in a noose, its rope extending into the boughs of the tree. "What the f—"

"Don't move, any of you!" a voice said from behind them.

The four of them with feet still on the ground turned and saw a man in jeans and a blue plaid shirt, with a mop of reddish-brown hair and a beard the same color but speckled with white. He was gripping a Remington hunting rifle, pointed right at them.

Alex twisted around and tried as best as he could to look dignified, which was not exactly easy, given the circumstances. "Kevin Hartinger?"

"That's me," the man said.

"My name is Alex Shephard—"

"Save it, Marine. I heard you the first time."

"Then you know why we're here, Sir."

"I surely do, son. I surely do."

Hartinger pivoted and pointed the rifle in Alex's direction. Kate shouted, "Stop!" as Hoffman, Vasquez, and Chan reached for the knives in their belts. Before they could act, Hartinger pulled the trigger. The bullet flew out and pierced right through the rope holding Alex. He fell hard and heavy onto the ground.

Hartinger put down his rifle and let out a loud laugh. The others just stared at him as Kate helped Alex to his feet.

Hartinger's laughter finally subsided. He wiped his eyes and grinned. "Sorry about that, folks. They don't let me have Internet up here, so I have to make my own fun."

* * *

Twenty minutes later, they were all huddled around a table inside Hartinger's shack. He had given them all bottles of water, which they gulped down, and they wasted no time stuffing their faces with the dried meats he put in front of them.

"What are we eating here?" Kate asked.

"Mostly rabbit. Some raccoon, a few possums."

"After scavenging for canned vegetables, this is a five-star meal, sir," Vasquez said, tearing into one of the strips.

"I got to say, Mr. Hartinger," Hoffman said as he shoveled food into his mouth, "I'm pretty damn impressed with the booby traps you got here. The way you Ewok-ed Shephard . . . that was some vintage old school trickery, sir. Very elegant."

"What are you talking about, bro?" Chan asked.

"Uh, a little flick called *Return of the Jedi*? How am I the only person here with an education in the classics? Han Solo and the other rebels got captured by the Ewoks with a rope trap tied to a tree."

"As it happens, that was my inspiration," Hartinger said.

Hoffman grinned. "I knew it," he said, chewing on his meat.

Kate ate her food in record time. "Mr. Hartinger—"

"You're not military, are you?"

She blinked. "No, I'm a civilian."

"Then you can go ahead and call me Kevin, little lady."

"Okay, Kevin. Do you have any medical supplies? We have some wounded here."

"I surely do." Hartinger rose and went to a cabinet, and produced several kits with red crosses on them. He handed them to Kate, who opened them all and scavenged through them.

"This'll do. Okay, Natalia, let's suture you up."

Vasquez rolled up the leg of her shorts, exposing the wound, which had turned a nasty shade of purple around the duct tape.

"Ready for some good news?" Kate said. "Our new friend here has a decent supply of morphine."

"Fuck, yes," Vasquez responded. "Do me up, Doc."

As Kate injected Vasquez and went to work, Alex turned to Hartinger.

"So," he said, "let's talk Seraphim."

"Ah, yes," Hartinger responded. "The highest choir of angels."

"I don't know what you heard, sir, but the Seraphim ain't no angels," Chan said.

"Actually, Corporal," Hartinger said, "they kinda are."

They all looked at each other.

"I'm confused," Hoffman said.

"Well, son, here's what I know. You've no doubt heard all the crazy, whacked-out conspiracy theories about aliens visiting the ancient people of the earth."

"You mean like on that TV show on the History Network?" Hoffman said.

"Yeah. Ridiculous, right? Also pretty much 100% true."

"You've got to be shitting me," Alex said.

"From what we understand, the Seraphim were visiting the earth when we were still crawling out of the primordial swamp and trying to figure out how to stand on two legs. We've never been alone in the universe. But the top of the top of the topmost levels of government—

the world over—collectively decided that humanity was not quite ready for that news."

"Who the fuck makes that kind of decision?" Vasquez said, slamming her fist on the table. She watched, numbed, as Kate began to stitch her wound back together.

"Whoever it is, they're way above my pay grade," Hartinger responded. "But that was the consensus. And so, the number of Americans who knew about the Seraphim was less than you could fit in a hotel lobby. But lucky me, I was one of them."

"Brady told us you had a third of vital information," Alex said. "What was he referring to?"

"That would be 31.1300," Hartinger said.

Alex squinted. "Am I supposed to know what that means?"

"Well, I've never been much of a cartographer," Hartinger said, "but to me it sounds a lot like one half of a set of coordinates."

"But there's no direction attached," Alex said.

"No, there is not. Which I imagine has something to do with this intel being split into three sections."

Alex leaned back in his chair. "I don't suppose you have any idea about where the coordinates would lead us, once they're complete?"

"Well, if they told me that, what would be the point of splitting up the intel in the first place?" Hartinger said.

Alex sighed and rubbed his eyes. "Saving the world is hard," he groaned.

CHAPTER 4

After a few hours of sleep, they hit the road in pursuit of the second sleeper agent. Hoffman, Vasquez, and Chan took the SUV they had acquired while Alex and Kate sat with Hartinger in his armored M998 Humvee. In Missouri, they soared up I-49, about a hundred miles south of Kansas City. They were headed toward the Niobrara River, part of a national park in Nebraska.

"What's with the national parks?" Kate asked.

Hartinger responded, "The American government wanted to make sure we were on protected land. Easier to keep us out of the way, given how structured the parks are, little lady."

"Agent Hartinger, I can't help but notice you never called Vasquez 'little lady.' Is it because she's military and I'm civilian?"

"I reckon it probably is."

"Well, why don't we just pretend I'm military, then."

"Roger that, ma'am."

"So who's this next agent we're activating?" Alex asked. He had one of Hartinger's assault rifles locked and loaded, aimed at the sky, prepared in case any Seraphim happened to drop on them out of the blue. As Hartinger was driving, Kate navigated and handled the documents.

"You probably already know, don't you, Kevin?"

Hartinger shook his head. "No, ma'am. I was informed there were two other agents, but we never met or saw each other's faces."

"Why is that?"

"In case one of us was captured, we wouldn't be able to give out identifying information regarding the other agents."

"Wow," Kate said, flipping through the paperwork. "Well, we're looking for a guy by the name of Fisher Matthews. He was one of the military's top tech guys. Looks like he was plucked right out of NASA, which has kind of an irony to it, I guess."

Alex chuckled.

"Thirty-six years old. British parents. First generation of his family born in America. Uh . . . what else? Did a tour of duty in Afghanistan . . . there's really not that much information."

"That's standard," Hartinger said. "Uncle Sam keeps intel on all of his Special Forces agents pretty damn close to the vest."

"So he's a tech guy living out in a national park with no Internet," Alex said. "I wonder if he'll be cranky—*shit!*"

The sky, which had been empty, suddenly boasted five Seraphim flying straight toward them. Alex took aim and blasted several rounds at them. In the car behind them, he heard shots ringing out as well.

"How many?" Hartinger asked.

"Five, loose formation." The Seraphim spread out to make a more difficult target.

"Bastards," Hartinger grumbled.

"Incoming!" Alex yelled as he saw one of the Seraphim's hand begin to glow. Sure enough, one second later a beam shot out of that hand and landed right where they would have been, had Hartinger not swerved the Humvee to the side at the last possible moment. The road crumbled into a charred hole on impact with the beam.

Alex took a deep breath, aimed, and fired, catching one of the Seraphim between the eyes. Its head reared back, spraying blood behind it. Now lifeless, but still buoyed up by its jet pack, the Seraphim hung there in the sky, motionless, like something out of a grotesque surrealist painting.

The other four Seraphim swooped away, but two of them were caught by the gunfire coming from the other car. *Most likely Chan,* Alex thought. He was the best marksman out of all of them, even with a weapon as cumbersome as an M16.

Two Seraphim left.

Hartinger gunned the engine and swerved the Humvee as another blast came from up high. The road sizzled and cracked, but they managed to evade it. Hoffman, Vasquez, and Chan, however, weren't so lucky.

The second beam came down and sliced right through their engine. Alex watched in horror as the SUV turned and flipped onto its side, skidding down the road, the crunch of metal on pavement squealing out a wretched refrain.

"No!" he shouted, letting loose another spray. Both Seraphim evaded his fire and retaliated with hand beams, cracking the road in front of them. Hartinger had no choice but to slam on the brake and whip the jeep to the side.

"Stay down, Kate! Keep your head low!" Alex yelled. Once the Humvee came to a stop, he leaped out of the vehicle, covering himself with blind fire and running over to the SUV. He chanced a look at the Seraphim and saw one of them take a hit—Hartinger was firing away with a handgun Alex didn't even know he had on him.

As he neared the SUV, he saw Vasquez crawling out the side door, now positioned as the top of the vehicle. Half of her face was covered in blood, and she had in her arms the combat shotgun she'd taken from Hartinger's cache.

"Shephard, *down!*" she screamed.

Without skipping a beat, Alex dropped onto the pavement, and Vasquez fired. He heard the sound of whistling above his head for an instant, then the catch of metal in flesh behind him. He turned and saw the last remaining Seraphim, hovering barely a foot above the ground, take the bullet directly in the chest. The force of the impact sent the shell straight through its body, blasting apart the jet pack on its back. Its flying mechanism disabled, it crashed backwards onto the road.

Alex ran over to the overturned SUV as Vasquez half-fell out of it. Once she hit the ground, she fell to one knee, crying in pain. Alex saw the wound on her leg had been reopened in the crash. He knelt down, but she waved him away.

"Check the guys," she told him through gritted teeth.

"Chan! Hoffman!" Alex called. He hoisted himself up and peered into the vehicle. Chan was conscious and moving, struggling to lift the unconscious Hoffman, holding him under his arms.

"I need a hand!" he called out to Shephard. Together, they managed to pull Hoffman out of the vehicle and place him gently down on the road. By then Hartinger and Kate had joined them. Hartinger helped Chan out of the vehicle as Kate knelt down at Hoffman's side.

Alex feverishly searched the sky around them, looking for more Seraphim. His heart pounded in his chest as he cocked his gun, determined to not let his guard down, even for an instant. The Seraphim were just so damn fast. The slightest millisecond of distraction could mean the difference between surviving their attack and not. Fortunately, they'd made it through this one.

"Oh, my God," Kate said behind him.

It was a tone he had never heard her voice take before. His back was to them, and something in her voice made him not want to turn around.

He heard them murmuring to each other. A whisper. Someone choked back a sob.

Don't turn around, he thought. They had made it through. They'd fought back. They'd beaten the Seraphim. Hoffman was just knocked out.

"Alex," Kate said. He could tell from her voice she was crying.

"No," he whispered. He continued staring at the sky, his gun aimed and ready.

"Alex," Kate said again.

Finally, he forced himself to turn around. They were all gathered around Hoffman, who lay on the pavement. He wasn't moving. Not even his chest, with the soft breath of sleep.

Kate wiped her eyes and looked up at Alex. "He's dead."

Alex bit his lip and shook his head. No. This wasn't fair. They'd beaten the Seraphim. They'd won. This wasn't . . .

"No," he said.

"He's gone, Alex."

Alex finally looked down at Hoffman's face. He wasn't sure he'd ever seen anything so still.

He then turned and marched over to where the last Seraphim lay. It was dead, a bowling-ball-sized cavity in its chest. But that wasn't good enough. Alex took aim and unloaded what was left of the magazine into the thing's face. When he was out of ammunition, he screamed and kicked the shredded body. He knew he could no longer hurt it, but kicking it just felt so *good*. But then he felt arms wrap around him and pull him back, and barely registered that it was Chan.

"Come on, bro, we got to get moving," Chan said.

Alex shrugged him off. "I got it. I know," he said.

They walked back to the rest of the group. Hartinger had pulled a sheet out of his Humvee and laid it over Hoffman's body. He stood near it, looking tense.

"We don't have the time to bury him, son. We got to hightail it out of here. Pronto."

"Yes, sir," Alex said. Tactics. The mission. Of course.

His whole body felt numb as he climbed into the Humvee. As they took off, he allowed himself one last look behind them, at Hoffman's body covered in a sheet. The least respectful funeral possible for a good man and a good marine.

Alex tightened his grip on the assault rifle, thinking only about how good it would feel to blast apart a few hundred more Seraphim.

* * *

They were all silent as they rode into Niobrara State Park. They hadn't spoken much since the attack on the highway—there didn't really seem to be that much to say. Alex sat in the front passenger seat as Hartinger drove, and he stared blankly at the trees as they passed. He tried to focus on the beauty of nature all around them, of Mother Earth in all her spectacular glory.

But all he could see was Hoffman's body under a sheet, abandoned on the highway, left to the elements and whatever scavengers might come sniffing around. No one deserved an end like that. He wouldn't have wished it on his worst enemy, and here he just watched it happen to one of his best friends.

He clenched his fist. He would make the Seraphim pay.

They soon approached the bridge that took them over the Niobrara River. Once they were on it, Alex grew anxious. He scanned the sky in all directions. "I think you should floor it, sir," he said to Hartinger.

"Don't have to tell me twice, Corporal," Hartinger responded, and gunned the engine. They shot like a bullet across the bridge, and Alex heard Kate let out a sigh of relief once they were on solid land again. They were all still rattled by the attack, and the bridge felt just a little too vulnerable for comfort. The Seraphim had, after all, proven they could just appear suddenly without warning.

Not exactly an aspect one looks for in an enemy.

They drove into the park, over a vast field littered here and there with picnic tables and one or two grills. It was clearly a place meant for family fun. But its sheer size, combined with its utter emptiness made for an eerie sight.

"Is it time for more morphine?" Vasquez grunted. She had been in bad shape ever since the attack. In addition to the reopened wound on her leg, she had also suffered a nasty laceration on her forehead and a dislocated shoulder.

"Not yet," Kate said. "Hold tight, Natalia. I know it sucks, but we've got to ration it as much as we can. Don't know when we're getting a new supply."

Vasquez bit her lip, nodded, and turned to look out the window.

They soon reached the bank of the Niobrara River, and Hartinger killed the engine. "This is where we get out," he said.

Confused, Chan looked around. "There aren't any buildings around besides that shed over there. Where does this guy live?"

"That would be a few miles downriver, son," Hartinger said.

"You've got to be fucking kidding me," Vasquez grumbled.

They all climbed out of the car as Hartinger ducked into the shed Chan had observed. A minute later he emerged with a large bundle of gray plastic and an electric pump.

"Everyone grab an oar," he said. "It's whitewater time."

Alex realized the plastic bundle was an inflatable raft and felt a stab of misery. The air was getting cooler, and the last thing he wanted was to get soaking wet. But he was a marine, and currently uninjured for the most part, so he took that part of him that wanted to complain and stuffed it into a tiny box in the corner of his brain. Complaining was for civilians, he told himself, and even Kate—the only civilian among them—barely made a peep no matter how tired or hurt she was. He had a job to do now, so there was no choice but to do it.

In no time at all they were on the river, floating down the relatively calm water. Alex breathed a sigh of relief. Hartinger's declaration of whitewater seemed to be a healthy exaggeration. Then they rounded a bend, and he saw what lay ahead of him.

God damn it, he thought.

Up ahead, the water dropped off over a sharp rocky decline. The fall wasn't much—maybe four or five feet from the looks of it. Nothing life-threatening, but with Vasquez and Chan as banged up as they were, it wasn't going to be pretty.

"Hold tight, guys," Alex said.

Chan nodded, and Vasquez did the same. They worked as one to angle themselves correctly facing downstream. Soon they were three feet away . . . two . . . one . . .

The sound of the water roared up at them as the tip of their raft went over. Kate screamed and clutched the side. Alex braced himself as they dropped into open air, only to land hard as they smacked into the water once again. Fortunately, they didn't capsize, and he turned back to Vasquez and Chan. Wet and miserable, both marines gave him the thumbs up.

They traveled about a mile farther downriver, and then Hartinger abruptly ordered that they ground themselves on the bank. Alex looked toward land and saw a tiny cabin, no more than a shack, deep in the wooded area beyond.

"Déjà vu," Kate said.

"What do you mean, ma'am?" Hartinger asked.

"This is a lot like when we approached your place, Kevin."

"No, ma'am, I must respectfully disagree. My setup was much nicer."

Alex started to walk towards the cabin, then stopped. "It just occurred to me that the last time I took point, I ended up hanging upside down from a tree. Perhaps you'd like to make first contact, sir?"

"Will do, son."

Hartinger stepped in front of him and called out, "Agent Matthews! This is Agent Kevin Hartinger. Code Three Tango Charlie Five Niner Bravo Delta."

"What the hell was that?" Kate asked.

"Clearance code," Alex whispered to her. "So Matthews'll know he's legit."

Then they all heard it at the same time: the click of a gun from above them. Immediately Hartinger and the three marines snapped their weapons up in the direction of the sound. There, perched in the tree branches above them, was a gangly man of medium height, dressed in pants and a jacket that camouflaged him perfectly among the trees. He held a hunting rifle across his lap, and a stub of a cigarette hung from his lips.

"At ease!" he called out.

"Fisher Matthews?" Hartinger said.

"That's me," the man said. He slung the rifle over his back and scurried down the tree, jumping the last five feet. He dropped the cigarette and squashed it with his boot. "So, you're one of my counterparts," he said to Hartinger. "Pleasure to meet you."

Hartinger shook his hand. "Same."

Matthews turned to the rest of them. "You all look like shit warmed over. Let's get you dried up and fed."

As they all moved toward his cabin, Matthews said, "You know, I've been waiting for someone to come for weeks. Nice to see other faces. Well, other *human* faces, anyway."

"There's been Seraphim activity here, sir?" Alex said.

"Some," Matthews said. "Not for at least a week or so."

"How frequently were their visits?" Hartinger asked.

"Since the invasion began I spotted them three times. One I killed. The second time it was two of them. They did a flyby but didn't see me. The third was . . . interesting."

"How so?"

"Follow me."

Matthews led them to his cabin and pushed the door open. They all crammed into the tiny space, and once they were all in, Matthews opened a closet door and removed an oddly shaped machine. It was tubular in shape, open on both sides, and clearly damaged.

Alex leaned down close to it. "Wait a minute. Is that . . .?"

"One of the Seraphim's jet packs," Matthews said. "One of them showed up practically at my doorstep. It was already injured, probably ran into some humans and got the raw end of a firefight. It didn't take much to finish her off."

"Her?" Kate asked.

"It wasn't until I saw her up close that I realized she was female. Outwardly they don't look that different than males, especially given the lack of any hair, though they have the same specific biological variations as humans from what I saw. But this female was just as large as the males, seemed just as strong, etcetera, so it's possible that goes for all of them."

"Evolutionary biologists have postulated that, as humans evolve, the sexes will become much more similar in appearance," Kate said. "Maybe that already happened for the Seraphim."

"Seems that way," Matthews said. "Anyway, her pack was already heavily damaged, but I wanted to see if I could figure out how it works. The fact that they're airborne is their biggest advantage, obviously. Like the difference between armed knights on horseback versus foot soldiers, only ten times as extreme. I was hoping that if I could figure out how it works, we could replicate the technology and get some wings of our own."

"Any luck?" Alex asked.

"The device is too damaged. If I wasn't already starting off with alien technology, I might be able to extrapolate a little better, but as it stands now . . . no."

"That's a damn shame," Alex said. "I'd love to strap on a jet pack and blow every last one of those fuckers back to hell."

Before he could stop himself, he pounded his fist on the table.

"Alex," Kate said, putting a hand on his shoulder.

"You'll have to excuse us, Matthews," Hartinger said. "These people lost one of their own on the way over here. A good marine."

"That's a shame," Matthews said. "You have my condolences."

"Thank you, sir," Alex said.

"Well, seeing as how you're all soaking wet, why don't you take turns using my shower? There are towels in the bathroom. I've got some food I can heat up."

"That sounds great, sir," Alex said. "Much obliged."

* * *

When they were all cleaned up, they squeezed around Matthews' table for a meal of microwaved venison and spinach. The agent looked at all of them and laughed. "You know," he said, "this is the most interaction I've had with people in quite some time."

"We talking months or years?" Chan asked.

"Years," Hartinger and Matthews said in unison.

Kate laughed at that, then quickly stifled it as she surveyed the grim faces. "Sorry," she said. "So, Agent Matthews, um, Kevin told us his third of the secret info thing, which sounded like part of some kind of coordinates. What was it you were given?"

"You get right to the point, there, don't you, ma'am?"

"Well, we've kind of been through a lot in the past few days."

Matthews rubbed his chin, which was covered with two-day-old stubble. "Coordinates, huh? I thought that's what it might be. Or partially, anyway. The bit of intel they had me memorize was just 3N, 9W."

"That's a little vague," Chan said.

"Hmm," Hartinger said. "My intel fragment was 31.1300. So I think we can now operate under the assumption that the first half of the coordinates is 31.1300 degrees north."

"Narrows it down some, but that's still a lot of longitude to account for," Matthews said.

"Good thing we know where the third sleeper agent is," Alex said.

Matthews chuckled. "Never did like the term sleeper agent. Makes me sound like a Russian spy."

Hartinger laughed. "Instead of a weirdo living in the woods by himself?"

"Exactly." Matthews wiped his mouth with a napkin. "We can set out tomorrow at first light to get our final agent. Hartinger, I assume you briefed these people on the backstory of our new friends?"

"Yes, indeed."

"I still can't believe the government knew about these things," Kate said.

"Not just the American government, ma'am," Matthews said. "This was decided by a counsel composed of many nations."

"So a conspiracy. What do you know? The nut bags were right all along."

"In my experience, ma'am," Matthews said, leaning back in his chair, "they usually are."

* * *

Later that night, Alex awoke with a start. He looked at his watch and saw that it was just after 3:00 a.m. He waited for his eyes to adjust to the dim light, then looked around the room. Matthews had rolled out what sheets he had, and the rest slept with their packs as pillows. He made out the sleeping form of Matthews, Hartinger, Vasquez, and Kate beside him.

Chan, he knew, was taking his turn keeping watch.

Might as well go relieve him, Alex thought. *No use both of us being awake.*

Alex silently rose and walked out the door of the cabin. He looked around but couldn't see Chan anywhere.

"Chan?" he called out.

"Here, man," Chan replied, his voice carrying through the darkness.

Alex followed the sound of his voice to a small clearing about twenty meters away from the house. His buddy was standing still, hand on his sidearm at his hip, scanning the sky.

"Clear skies so far?" Alex asked.

"So far." Chan scowled. "Is it wrong that a part of me was hoping to see one of them, just so I could shoot it down?"

"Nope. Pretty much feel the same way myself."

"Yeah, I figured from the way you turned the dead one on the highway into ground beef."

Alex nodded. "Yeah."

Chan took a deep breath. "You're a Christian, right?"

Alex blinked in surprise. In all his time with Chan, Vasquez, and Hoffman, no one had ever brought up what higher power they believed in. It just wasn't something they ever talked about. Hoffman had once briefly mentioned his bar mitzvah, but that was it.

"Yeah," he said.

"I caught sight of your cross once," Chan explained. "What do you think? Is this some kind of punishment for the wickedness of mankind?"

"No," Alex said. "I don't believe that for a second."

"Why not?"

"Because there's too much good in the world. Or there *was*, anyway. I don't think God would punish everyone for the sins of some."

"What about the flood, though? Or Sodom and Gomorrah?"

"That was Old Testament."

"Oh. Right. Before Jesus."

"Yeah. Why? What do you believe?"

Chan sighed. "Honestly? Nothing. My parents are Taoists, tried to bring me up the same way, but it didn't stick. A lot of it's about action through nonaction." Chan patted his gun. "Nonaction isn't something I'm too down with. I like to act. Especially these days."

Alex looked at his buddy. "Why are you asking me about religion now?" he asked.

"Well, we've kind of got the end times on our hands. I figure if there's a time to talk about it, it's probably now."

Alex chuckled. "Well, you got a point there."

"Must be nice, though. Believing in something."

"It gives me comfort."

"You believe in heaven, right? All that?"

"Yeah."

Chan nodded. "Must be nice," he said again.

Alex remembered something he learned in Basic about surviving a crisis. Some people, especially trained military, developed a sort of switch they could flip in horrible or dangerous situations, such as when they had to endure torture. They became a machine, unemotional, as a way to cope. The part of the brain that processes anguish and pain turns off, to avoid a total mental breakdown. But even the most hardened warriors could only last so long before that switch started to try to flip back, and that's where the real struggle was. And Alex saw this struggle happening all over Chan's face.

"Chan," he said gently, "listen, if you need—"

Chan suddenly brought his finger to his mouth and inclined his head, listening. Alex pivoted around, scanning the area. His pulse began to beat rapidly. He didn't hear anything, but he could feel it. Something was off.

They both drew their sidearms. They locked eyes, silently communicating their plan. Then they moved back to back, aiming out into the darkness. Alex held his breath.

A minute passed. Two. Three. Nothing happened.

Maybe they had imagined—

"Fuck!" Chan cried.

Alex whipped his head in the direction Chan was facing just in time to see the Seraphim bound out of the darkness and snatch up his friend. Chan aimed his gun right at the alien's temple, but it quickly grabbed the weapon out of his hand and flung it far off into the trees.

"Chan!" Alex shouted. He tried to find an opening to fire at the Seraphim, but there was too high a risk of hitting Chan. Then the Seraphim took flight, soaring into the sky, its ghostly wings catching the moonlight, just barely there. It turned its back to Alex, and that's when he opened fire, getting three bullets right into its jet pack. He heard a sharp mechanical fizzle, and the Seraphim began losing altitude. In silhouette, he saw Chan reach for his knife, pull it out of its holster on his thigh, and jam it into the creature's neck.

Alex watched as the two of them crashed down about a hundred meters farther into the woods. He had to make a split-second decision: go back to the cabin and get help, or go to Chan alone. Realizing he might not have a second to spare to save his friend, he bounded into the trees.

He got to the spot where he had seen them go down, but in the darkness, he couldn't see anything. Then suddenly he made out a shape lying a little bit farther away, too small to be a Seraphim. It had to be Chan.

He took two steps toward him when what felt like a Mack truck hit him from the side. He immediately went down, hitting the ground hard, and felt the breath go out of him. He looked up and saw the Seraphim hovering above him. It was bleeding profusely out of the gash that Chan had made in its neck, and it was wobbling slightly. It was hurt, but Alex knew better than to underestimate it, especially as it raised its arm high in the air. It brought the hovering fist down fast, but Alex rolled out from underneath, dodging the blow that pounded a dent into the earth.

Alex scrabbled backwards on his hands and feet, trying to put distance between himself and the Seraphim, but it leapt on him, pushed his chest down hard, and raised its arm again. Alex's hand found a rock, which he immediately grasped. He struck the creature in its face with as much force as he could muster.

The Seraphim cried out in pain, and even through his fear Alex realized that now he knew they could make noise, after all. And there was no sound he would rather hear than that creature screaming in pain.

Alex hit it again, this time slamming the rock right against the wound on the Seraphim's neck. More blood poured out. Alex went to strike it once again with the rock, but the thing grasped it with its larger hand and flung it away. Alex grabbed the creature's other arm with both hands and pulled up his legs, wrapping them around its neck. He hooked one foot behind his other knee and squeezed as hard as he could, hoping the triangle choke technique would work as well on an alien as it had on the sparring opponents he took on during basic training.

The Seraphim staggered under the crushing hold, and for a moment Alex thought he might be subduing it. But then it tapped into some reserve of strength and got to its feet, lifting Alex off the ground. The creature reached a hand around one of Alex's ankles and pried him off, then flung him away. Alex soared through the air, stopping when he crashed into a tree. He hit it with his ribs and felt the air go out of him as he fell to the ground. He knew he couldn't even take a moment to collect himself, or it would be the last moment of his life.

Springing to his feet, he ignored the searing pain in his side and the lack of oxygen in his lungs, and braced himself as the Seraphim launched itself at him once again. Alex went low, crouching down and tackling the alien around the waist, keeping one foot on the ground and pushing himself off the tree with the other. His tactic worked, and the Seraphim collapsed with him on top. He rained down punches on its face and throat, but it barely seemed to feel the blows. The Seraphim struck at Alex with the back of its hand, knocking him onto his back.

Dazed, Alex lay on the ground for a moment, vaguely aware of the Seraphim rising beside him. As quick as he could, he reached down to his thigh and unholstered his knife. When the Seraphim dove at him, Alex slammed the knife as hard as he could in its direction, not even seeing where he was aiming the weapon. He felt it connect, but then the knife was ripped out of his hand.

The knife had been his last hope. He closed his eyes, waiting for the death strike.

It never came.

Hesitantly, Alex opened one eye. Once the world stopped spinning, he looked to his side and saw the unmoving form of the Seraphim, his knife sticking out the side of its temple, its eerie white eyes wide open, blood leaking from the wound in its head and the corner of its mouth.

The fight was over.

Alex gave himself a minute to catch his breath, then painfully sat up. His ribs felt like they were on fire. He looked over to where Chan lay and saw he was face down on the ground, still not moving. *Please, God, let him just be unconscious,* Alex prayed.

He dragged himself to his feet, then staggered over to Chan. He turned his friend over, saw the unnatural twist in his neck, the blood coming out of his ears. He put his fingers to Chan's throat. No pulse. He put his ear against Chan's chest and listened for a heartbeat. Nothing.

Alex looked from his dead friend to the Seraphim twenty feet away. For the first time since the invasion began, he put his face in his hands and cried.

* * *

Twenty-four hours later, they were again on the road. No one had spoken much since Alex had reported his fight with the Seraphim. The group quickly dug a grave and buried Chan in the forest, then split the troop between the two Humvees belonging to Hartinger and Matthews. They were all anxious to leave the place where a Seraphim had died, lest they encounter any of its friends who might be looking for it.

They drove west, to Sego Canyon in Utah, where the last of the agents, a man named Jack Mason, was located. Alex and Kate sat in the back of Matthews' vehicle. Alex was looking out the window when he felt her slide her hand into his. "Are you all right?" she asked.

He just shook his head.

She leaned against him. Her warmth was a comfort, but he couldn't stop seeing the dead faces of Chan and Hoffman.

Soon they arrived in Sego. Mason lived in a small cabin in an abandoned town on the side of a mountain, which was covered in petroglyphs from as far back as 6000 BC. The primitive rock drawings depicted small human beings cowering before what looked like large, humanoid shapes with wavy lines coming out of their backs.

"All this time," Vasquez muttered. "They've been visiting us all this fucking time."

"Let's just keep moving," Hartinger said.

When they found Mason's cabin, they called out his name, but there was no response. They decided to enter, with Hartinger taking the lead. From inside, Alex heard him mutter, "God damn it."

Alex entered and was met with a hideous sight. Mason was lying on the ground in a pool of his own blood. The smell indicated he'd been dead for days.

"They got here first," Vasquez said.

"Look at this," Hartinger said. He crouched down next to the body. Alex saw that Mason's hand was lying in his own blood, and there were markings on the floor right past the pool. Red markings.

He had written something in his own blood.

When Kate realized this, she looked away, biting her lip. Alex patted her shoulder. "What does it say?" he asked.

"97.7800," Hartinger said.

"Poor bastard. Now we got our coordinates, at least," Matthews said. "Hand me the map?"

He spread the map out on a nearby table and studied it for a moment. "Fort Hood," he said. "Fort Hood in Texas. That's where we need to go. That's where we'll finally get some answers as to what in the holy hell is happening."

2109

"That's it?" the young man said. "All that traveling and death just to end up at another military base?"

"Fort Hood was no ordinary military base," the old man said. He coughed a little, then pulled a handkerchief out of his pocket and dabbed at the corner of his mouth. "Say, could I have another whiskey?"

The younger man's fingers danced across the mech-table, and soon a full glass was placed in front of the old man. He took a sip, savoring the taste, before setting it down again and eyeing the younger man across the table.

"Fort Hood," he said, "operated in the standard base fashion, or at least that's what it did on the surface level. And I'm using that phrase literally. The level that was on the surface of the earth was a regular military base. But right in the middle of the base was a very unassuming custodial closet, and underneath the false bottom of that closet was a hatch, which led to something else entirely."

"What?"

"Have you heard of Area 51? Roswell?"

"Of course, but those rumors had already been debunked by the time the Seraphim invaded, hadn't they?"

The old man laughed and leaned back in his chair. "Well, someone certainly knows his history. Yes, there were wild rumors about the American government hiding alien bodies and ruins of spacecrafts and whatnot. But any feisty kid with an Internet connection could figure out that these rumors were bogus, and Area 51 wasn't nearly as interesting as people made it out to be. And therein lies the genius."

"I don't follow."

"The government absolutely kept alien bodies and ships for scientific study. But rather than just denying it, they also set up Area 51 as a decoy site. Since it was so easily debunked, no one took the rumors seriously. And so, therefore, no one went looking just one state over in Texas, where the real hangars with extraterrestrial material were held."

The younger man shook his head as he absorbed the information. "That's pretty diabolical," he said.

"Well, that's a matter of opinion. But one thing's for sure—it worked. And now, at last, we come to why the Seraphim decided to invade Earth in the first place."

CHAPTER 5

They all stood and looked down curiously at the hatch.

"This has got to be a freakin' joke," Vasquez said.

"No, ma'am," Hartinger said. "Matthews and I were both given the same orders. If we're ever in the position where we're brought to the location our intel fragments indicate, we're to move to the center of said location and descend past the false bottom. This closet is right in the center of Fort Hood, and you've seen the false bottom."

"Yeah, I got it," Vasquez said. "Well, let's open it up."

"Roger that," Alex said. The hatch was just a steel door with a circular turning mechanism, so he grabbed the wheel with both hands, and with great effort managed to turn it a full ninety degrees. There was a click, and he opened it up to discover a ladder leading down into a tight cement hallway, dimly lit.

"Here goes nothing," he said. He descended the ladder. Just as his foot was about to hit the floor, he heard a voice from behind him.

"Well, no wings. So I reckon that means you're a friendly."

He turned and saw a young man, probably no more than twenty, dressed in army fatigues and holding a gun pointed right at him. He looked almost comical gripping the weapon—with his red hair and freckles, he looked more like an Archie comic book character than a soldier.

"You want to lower that sidearm, seeing as how we're such good friends?" Alex asked.

The boy re-holstered his weapon. "Right. Sorry. We're a little on edge."

"You don't say." He looked up through the hatch to the others. "It's cool!" he shouted.

"How many you got with you?" the boy asked.

"Four more. A fellow marine, two CIA, and a civilian." Alex extended his hand. "Alex Shephard. Lance corporal. U.S. Marines."

The boy shook it. "Pratt, sir. Private second class."

"What's your first name, Pratt?"

"Richie."

"Richie, who's in charge around here?"

"That would be Sergeant Major Conners, sir."

"Well, Richie . . . take us to your leader."

Once they were all down the ladder, Alex and the others followed Richie through a series of winding hallways until at last they reached the door to an office. It was a barebones operation: blank gray walls surrounding a desk with a computer and a few chairs. Seated at the desk was a man of about sixty. He looked haggard, with lines around his eyes, and it had been a few days since he'd last shaved.

He looked up when he saw Richie leading the group into his office. "What's going on? Who're these guys?"

"Sir," Richie said, "they just came in through the hatch."

Hartinger and Matthews stepped forward. "Sergeant, I'm Kevin Hartinger and this is my counterpart Fisher Matthews. We were assigned sleeper duty with the CIA, given intel that led us here."

"Sergeant Major Nick Conners." The man rose and shook hands with the two agents, and then eyed the rest of them. "And you are?"

Alex stepped forward. "Lance Corporals Alex Shephard and Natalia Vasquez. This is my fiancée, Kate Riley. She's civilian but has medical training."

Upon hearing that, Conners brightened a bit. "Good. We're in need of medics. Why don't you three go with Richie and get settled in while the agents and I discuss certain matters?"

Hartinger put a hand up. "If it's all right with you, Sergeant, these people were responsible for activating us, and the effort cost them the lives of two of their fellow marines. I'd say they've earned the right to hear just what the fuck on God's green earth is going on. Respectfully speaking, of course."

Conners nodded. "Times like these, protocol doesn't have quite the same weight as it did in the past. If you three want to stay, that's fine by me."

"Thank you, sir," Alex said.

"Dismissed, Private."

Richie nodded and took his leave.

Conners sat back down. "Well, I'll brief you as much as I can, with the intel we currently have. It's not much, but it's something. As I'm sure you know, the Seraphim have been a part of Earth's history as long as humanity's been able to scribble down pictures on caves, and probably longer. They're an old race. How old exactly, we're not sure. But our guess is that they were already flying around in spaceships when we were crawling out of the primordial ooze on our bellies. They're incredibly advanced, obviously, particularly when it comes to bio-mechanical interfacing."

"You're referring to their flying mechanisms?" Matthews asked.

"The jet packs are just one example. Their entire bodies are outfitted with bionic implants. That's what gives them their strength, as well as their long lifespan. According to our sources, they can live as long as a thousand years, some even more."

"Jesus," Vasquez said.

"Any of you ever get close to them? Their skin gives off a kind of shimmer. That's the metal underneath."

"I've gotten close, sir," Alex said, "and I've seen what you're talking about."

"How close did you get, son?"

"Close enough to stab the fucker in the head, sir."

That got Conners' attention. "Explain."

"My buddy and I were attacked in the woods while activating Agent Matthews. There was a tussle. He didn't make it, but he got a lick in, stabbing the Seraphim in the neck. That hurt it, got it to slow down enough for me to fight it and take it out."

"Son," Conners said, "are you telling me that you killed a Seraphim in a goddamned fistfight?"

"Not completely. We had our knives, sir. But it was mostly hand to hand, yeah."

Conners chuckled and shook his head. "I have a number of men that are going to want to talk to you, Corporal. As far as I know, you're the only person we've got who's taken one of them out with anything less than gunfire."

"I'd be happy to talk to anyone, sir."

Matthews interrupted. "You were telling us about the bionics?"

"Ah, that's right," Conners said. "It really all comes down to that. You see, as a species they've apparently hit a bit of a glitch, which is why they showed themselves to us in the first place."

"What kind of a glitch?" Hartinger asked.

"Well, I'm no technological expert, but the way I understand it, it goes a little something like this. They've been tinkering with their own bodies for a few millennia, trying to improve everything about themselves with the bio-mech implants. But that came with a side effect: their bodies have started breaking down, specifically their blood, which has started to become incompatible with the implants. I guess they've evolved to a point where their bodies now need the tech to survive, but their own blood is poisoning them. So they need fresh blood, uncontaminated by any external machinery. Our blood."

A silence passed over the group. Finally, Alex spoke up. "They're . . . *transfusing* our blood into their bodies?"

"That's right, son."

Alex looked around. "But that seems impossible, doesn't it? How could our blood be compatible with theirs? We evolved on different planets."

Conners shrugged. "I thought so, too, but whether it makes sense to us or not, the end result is the same: they're imprisoning us to steal our blood. Our scientists have come up with a theory that maybe all intelligent life in the universe—seeing that now we know there's more out there besides us—is based on the same biological components, and that's why our blood would work with them. Unfortunately, the fact remains that what we don't know far surpasses what we do."

Kate shivered. "So all those people who've been taken . . ."

"Have either been drained, or are waiting to be drained."

"Oh, my God," Kate said. "Those poor people . . . do we know where they're keeping them?"

"We have some ideas, but we don't have nearly the manpower to recapture any of their prisoners. For now, our mission is pretty basic: stay alive. Accrue as much intel as we can. Learn how to blow these bastards back to whatever hell they crawled out of."

A silence fell over the group as they absorbed Conners' words. Alex realized that without anyone really saying it, they had all been operating under the assumption that their journey would lead them to some kind of answers. But no. All they had was an underground bunker full of humans who barely knew anything more than they did.

Alex felt sick inside, and as he locked eyes with Kate, he could see she was feeling the same.

* * *

"What do you think?" Alex asked.

They had been given tiny quarters, just a cramped room barely big enough for two narrow twin beds. With its blank gray walls and lack of windows, it looked as much like a prison cell as anything else. They had pushed the beds next to each other, and had barely laid down before they were both asleep. After an hour or so, Alex stirred awake and found Kate was already sitting up, hugging her knees to her chest. "What do I think about what?" she asked.

"About the whole blood thing. You think their intel is accurate?"

Kate ran her hands through her hair. "I mean, I'm not a biologist, and I have no idea about environments on any planet besides Earth. It does seem impossible, though—the odds of two beings evolving on separate planets being so biologically compatible. Statistically, that would have to be one in . . . I don't even know. One in a centillion. Or higher."

Alex furrowed his brow. "Yeah . . . unless . . ."

"Unless what?"

Alex had taken his shirt off when they slept, and his hand absentmindedly went to the cross lying against his chest. "Ever since the Seraphim showed up, I've been trying to reconcile so much in my head. About God. About why we're here. I mean, just their existence opens up so many doors, doors I probably don't even want to walk through. But this thing with the blood, if we really are compatible with them . . . doesn't it seem like that *has* to be by some kind of . . . design?"

"You mean the same God that created them created us?"

"Yeah."

Kate half-smiled and nodded. "That does make sense. I mean, sure, you could ask why a God who created such wonders would allow them to do something as horrible as this . . ."

"But you could also say that about any atrocity humans commit against each other."

"Exactly. Atrocities that have never been in short supply." She slid her hand into his, intertwined their fingers, and looked in his eyes, smiling. "I like that theory."

Just as Alex smiled back they heard shouting coming from the hall. He shook his head in misery. Shouting was never a good sign.

Kate rubbed her forehead. "I can't take any more disasters."

"I don't think we have a choice, babe. Let's go." He threw on his shirt and shoes, and the two of them exited the room.

There was a stream of people heading in one direction, so they followed the flow until they came to a large circular room, the size of a football field, covered on all sides with computer monitors. Everyone was crowding around one of the monitors on the far side of the room. Alex and Kate followed the herd, and saw Sergeant Major Conners standing among all the people. Alex looked up at the monitor and saw footage that appeared to be taken from an orbiting satellite. The earth was visible in the lower left-hand corner of the screen, and the rest was a blanket of stars across the vast expanse of space.

"What's happening?" Alex asked Conners.

"We have reports that more ships are entering the earth's atmosphere. They should be visible soon from the satellite."

"*More* Seraphim are coming? They decimated the human race in under a month. They don't really need reinforcements."

Conners said nothing and just stared at the screen. Alex did the same. He looked to his right and saw Hartinger and Matthews approaching them. There was a collective gasp from the crowd as three large ships passed into the frame, each of them a shiny bronze color on the exterior. Their appearance was unlike any of the previous ships the Seraphim had descended to Earth in.

"Shit," Conners grumbled, and turned and walked away from the crowd.

Alex, hearing him, turned and followed, with Kate beside him. Conners was walking fast and was already out of the room and away from the crowd before they caught up with him.

"Sergeant," Alex said. "What's going on?"

Conners stopped walking, and his shoulders raised in what was clearly a sigh. When he turned around, he looked pale and tired. "One more layer of hell is what's going on, son."

"What do you mean?"

"Those ships. We've seen them before. In surveillance footage."

"What are they?"

Conners looked away.

"Sergeant?" Alex said. "Why would the Seraphim be sending more ships?"

"They're not Seraphim, Corporal."

The words hung in the air between them for a long, horrible moment. Alex and Kate looked at each other.

"What are they?" Alex asked.

"Something new," Conners said, and turned and walked away.

PART TWO

The Book of
Revelation

CHAPTER 6

"**S**omething *new?*" Alex shouted. He raced down the hall after Conners, who turned sharply and stared daggers at him.

Conners looked back and said through gritted teeth, "Are you raising your voice at me, son?"

"I'm sorry, sir, but with all due respect, what in the fuck do you mean 'something new'?"

"Alex," Kate said, trying to calm him. She had just caught up to him.

But Alex ignored her and continued to question Conners. "Sir, if there's more to this than just the Seraphim, I'd say we've earned the right to hear about it."

Conners drew himself up to his full height, but he was still half a head shorter than Alex. Finally, he sighed, and his shoulders sagged. "Why don't you go ask your CIA buddies? They're the ones with the solid intel."

"Hartinger and Matthews? They know about this?"

"Unless you brought in some other black ops guys I don't know about. They're your men."

With that, he turned and walked away. Alex looked at Kate. "I can't believe this," he said. "I'm not sure I can take any more surprises."

She shook her head. "Me neither. But come on. Let's go find out what he meant."

They went back to the main room and looked through the crowd. In the last row of people who had lined up to look at the monitors, Hartinger and Matthews stood stoically watching the screen. Alex moved over to them and quietly said, "We need to talk."

The two agents looked at each other. For a moment, Alex worried they were going to refuse his request. But then, tired and resigned, they exchanged glances and nodded. "Let's go," Matthews said.

"I'm getting Natalia," Kate said. "She deserves to hear this, too."

Five minutes later, the five of them were huddled into Hartinger's quarters. Hartinger sat on one bed and Matthews sat on the other. The others stood.

"What did Conners mean when he said these ships were something new?" Alex asked without preamble.

Hartinger sighed. "I guess we should have told you this when you activated us," he said. "But we still weren't sure how much of the old protocols we were expected to follow."

"Is there *another* alien race?" Kate asked.

Hartinger and Matthews looked at one another. "Yes," Matthews said. "They're called the Malakhim. At first, our people assumed they were other Seraphim. But in recent decades, the Malakhim have proved a little less cagey than the Seraphim. They made contact. Recently."

"They made contact?" Alex said. "And you didn't think to mention this?"

"Orders," Hartinger said tersely. As explanations went, it wasn't much, but Alex knew that for agents of their level, orders were obeyed to the letter and without question.

"The Malakhim are thought to be friendly, but then, so were the Seraphim before the world went to shit," Matthews said. "When contact was made, it took us by surprise. Obviously it was kept top secret. The highest level of eyes-only, and even then, only a fraction of them."

"Which it sounds like you are," Vasquez said.

"Yes," Matthews said. "The Malakhim come from a nearby solar system, closer than the Seraphim. They also haven't been visiting us nearly as long. The reports state it's only been about the last three hundred years or so."

"Oh, is that all?" Kate said, rolling her eyes.

"There's some kind of history between the two species, but just what, we're not sure. The Malakhim resemble the Seraphim physically, but then so do we, kind of."

"Why is that, exactly?" Alex asked.

Matthews shrugged. "Who knows? Maybe the humanoid shape is the standard flow of evolution on every planet. But what we do know is that the Malakhim, like the Seraphim, are vastly superior to us technologically. And they're larger and stronger than us physically."

"Are they working with the Seraphim? Is that why they're here?" Alex asked.

"I don't know," Matthews said.

"But you seem like you do know a lot about them," Hartinger said suddenly. "More than me."

"Yes," Matthews said. "The last time contact was made, I was on the team." The others looked at him in stunned silence. "It was before I went dark," Matthews continued. "My last mission, actually. Myself and a team of three other agents went with the president and the top brass from NASA."

"The *president?*" Kate asked.

"That's the one, ma'am. It was some years ago. A Malakhim ship had landed not far from Washington and made contact through radio signals. The president insisted on being there."

"How does no one know about this?" Alex asked. "With satellites and cell phone cameras and all the types of surveillance these days, it just seems impossible."

"The Malakhim ships are capable of stealth beyond any of our own tech," Matthews said. "And there's long been an agreement between most countries of the world that any footage of alien craft is detained."

"But if it's recorded by a citizen on their own phone . . ." Kate said.

"Ma'am, with all due respect, you have no idea just how closely everything is monitored by the government. They can remotely wipe clean any footage taken anywhere and have done so on more than a few occasions."

Kate crossed her arms. "Jesus."

"The way I see it, there are two possibilities," Matthews said. "Either the Malakhim are here to help the Seraphim, or they're here to help us."

"Do we know which one of those possibilities is more likely?" Alex asked.

"Afraid not," Matthews said. "Like I said, we thought we knew the Seraphim, but then it turns out we were wrong, and that misinformation basically fucked the entire human race. We'll wait to see if the Malakhim contact us and then go from there."

Alex shook his head. "I don't like this. Any of this."

"Neither do I. But we don't exactly have a choice, now, do we?"

* * *

It turned out the wait was not long. Five hours after their ships appeared, the Malakhim broadcast a signal they had used in the past to contact the world leaders. The signal was picked up by an operative working at the base beneath Fort Hood, and Alex listened intently as Matthews and Hartinger were paged over the inter-com. Kate was in the infirmary helping the medics on duty, and Vasquez had gone to her quarters to rest. On hearing the agents' names, Alex darted up and ran to Conners' office.

Richie, the young private, stood outside the door, rifle in hand. "I'm sorry, Corporal, but you weren't summoned."

"I don't give a rat's ass about being summoned," Alex growled. "Let me pass. I'm in this."

Richie looked weary. "Please, sir. I'm sorry, but the sergeant has strict orders—"

"Conners!" Alex barked, and just as he did so Hartinger and Matthews rounded the corner.

"Shephard?" Hartinger said. "What are you doing?"

The door to Conners' office opened, and the sergeant major stood there, red-faced. "Who the hell is hollering my name?"

All four men stared at Alex, who suddenly felt self-conscious and silly, like a child begging to be seated at the grown-ups' table. But he had been in it for the long haul so far, and lost two of his men—two of his *friends*—in the process. He would be damned if they started excluding him now.

"I was, sir," Alex said. "I apologize. But whatever's going on, I deserve to be involved."

"Oh, is that right?" Conners said, puffing out his chest.

"Sergeant," Matthews said, "let him stay. Shephard has been instrumental in our getting here. We could use someone of his caliber."

Conners eyed Alex for a moment, then shrugged. "Fine. Let's go in my office."

He turned and walked back inside, and the others followed. Conners sat behind his desk and eyed the three men. "Let's keep this brief. A Malakhim ship has reached out to us. They want to meet."

"Could be a trap, sir," Hartinger said.

"No shit," Conners said. "But seeing as how Matthews here is the only one of us who's ever talked to these motherfuckers, I figure it'll be his call if we respond."

All eyes turned to Matthews. The agent scratched the back of his head for a moment. "I think we should do it, Sergeant," he said finally. "If we don't respond, we'll just stay in the exact same position as we're in now. If we do respond, there are two possibilities. One, it's a trap, so we lose a few men, myself included. Two, they want to help. It seems the possible benefit outweighs the risk."

"Sounds logical to me," Conners said. "Who do you want on your team?"

"Just Hartinger and the two marines we came with—Shephard here and Corporal Vasquez. Small, tight unit, plus the four of us have the benefit of having recently operated together in the field." Matthews stood silently, waiting for a response.

For a moment, Conners just looked at him. Then finally, he said, "All right, then. You leave in three hours."

Conners dismissed the men, and Alex walked back to the quarters he shared with Kate, unsure of how she would react to him putting himself in danger again so soon after they found shelter. But he was a marine, through and through, and she knew that.

Absentmindedly, he fingered the hilt of his knife, snug in its holster, the knife he'd used to kill the Seraphim. He wondered if he would have to use it again in the near future.

CHAPTER 7

They left the next morning. Alex held Kate in his arms and squeezed her close, and when he released her, there were tears on her face. "Why do you have to go?" she asked. "We just got to safety."

"We don't really know if this *is* safety, babe," he reminded her. "Sure, it's secure for now, but what happens when the Seraphim find out about this base? We have to see if maybe these other beings can help us."

"I hate this," she said, shaking her head. "We don't have any reason to believe they're any different than the first ones."

"But they might be. And that's all we've got right now."

Kate looked at the ground, and her shoulders sank. "Okay," she said. "All right. Go save the world. But do me a favor."

"What?"

"Be careful. Seriously. I know you've been all Rambo with the Seraphim, but how about you let the CIA guys take the risks in this mission?"

"Deal." He kissed her, then joined Vasquez, Hartinger, and Matthews in the armored truck that Conners provided them. As they pulled out, Alex looked through the back window and saw Kate waving to them. He waved back, watching her until she was as small as an ant in the distance.

Vasquez nudged him. "Don't you worry, man. She'll be safe in the base."

"Yeah," Alex said, wishing his voice sounded more certain. "I know."

"Estimated time of arrival is just under five hours," Matthews said. "We communicated to them to meet us in Texarkana. Obviously we didn't want to give up our location, so we figured there was enough white noise around there that it would throw the Mals off the scent if they tried to triangulate where we're holing up."

"The Mals," Alex repeated. "You guys are on nickname terms?"

"I wouldn't go that far, but I have had interaction with the leader we're going to meet. In fact, she was the one who led their convoy that met with the president."

"She?" Vasquez said.

"That's right," Matthews said. "Her name's Amitiel."

"That's weird," Alex said. "I never even thought about aliens having names."

"Everything has a name," Matthews said.

"On a scale of one to ten, how strongly do you believe this Amitiel and her posse will be friendly?" Hartinger asked.

"Based on when I met them last, and considering what we've learned about the Seraphim, I'd say about six."

Alex met eyes with Vasquez. "That's not too promising," Alex said.

"Well, like I said, we thought the Seraphim were at least benign, and they turned out to be a lot more demonic than angelic."

"Christ," Alex said. "We might really be walking straight into a trap."

"Maybe," Matthews said. "But my gut says no. It's not logical on their part. Why go through the trouble of back channels and covert comms if they just want to harvest our blood like the Seraphim? They'd just be getting four bodies. Doesn't make sense, given the effort involved, you know?"

"What should we expect, tech-wise? Do they have jet packs?" Vasquez asked.

"No," Matthews said. "Or, at least, they led us to believe they don't have them. They didn't seem to be quite as technologically advanced as the Seraphim. But again, we don't really know for sure. So we go in with one hand on our holsters at all times."

"Roger that," Alex said. "You don't have to tell me twice."

They drove on in silence for the next few hours. Alex knew his companions were probably thinking the same thing he was—they might very well be driving to their deaths. Sure, he had taken out a Seraphim in hand-to-hand combat, but it was just one, and his enemy was injured and without a functioning jet pack. And even then, Alex had delivered the killing blow blind. It wasn't really his skill that took out the Seraphim. It was luck.

* * *

By the time Matthews told them, they were five minutes away. The tension in the car became almost physically suffocating. Alex cracked open a window and felt the cool breeze on his face. He couldn't shake the feeling that no matter how this day played out, it was going to change everything one way or another.

They pulled to a stop next to what looked like an abandoned convenience store on the side of the road. Alex looked around at the vast expanse of dusty fields and blue sky, then back at the dilapidated building in front of them. It was the kind of place that looked like it hadn't changed a bit for decades. It was hard to believe what lay just inside its rickety door.

They all got out of the car. "Let me do all the talking," Matthews said. "And look sharp, but try not to seem hostile."

"After all the shit we've been through, I think we pretty much earned the right to be a little hostile," Vasquez said.

"I mean it, Vasquez. We don't want to spook them on the chance that they're friendly."

Vasquez frowned, but nodded.

"Ready?" Matthews said.

When they all gave him the thumbs-up, Matthews walked up to the door and pushed it open, then disappeared into the darkness inside. Alex took a deep breath and followed Hartinger in, with Vasquez taking the rear. It took a minute for his eyes to adjust to the lack of light, but even before they did, he knew they weren't alone.

When he could finally make out shapes in the darkness, he saw them. Standing in a straight line, with one of them in front. They were all giants, between seven and eight feet tall, long-limbed and bald. They wore tight-fitting clothes of a metallic grayish-blue hue that covered their whole bodies except for their heads. They looked like the Seraphim, complete with the white eyes, but Alex was relieved to see no ghost of wings behind them. They were just as locked to the earth as he and his companions were. If they attacked, at least the playing field would be slightly more level.

"Amitiel," Matthews said.

There was a stirring among the aliens, and the one standing in front took a step forward. As she did, Alex, Vasquez, and Hartinger all reflexively stepped back and brought a hand to their weapons.

"Fisher Matthews. Greetings. There is no need for caution," the alien said. Her voice was deeper than an average human woman's register, and yet it was smooth and detached, like an automated computer voice. Its otherworldliness sent shivers up Alex's spine.

"We might feel less cautious if we weren't so out-numbered," Matthews said. He kept his voice soft and level.

Amitiel inclined her head, and turned to the pha-lanx of Malakhim behind her. "All of you, please retreat to the ship."

As one, the line turned and exited the building through a back door. Alex watched them go, moving silently through the darkness. When they were gone, Amitiel approached them but kept a safe distance of about ten feet.

"Now the greater numbers are yours," she said.

"Thank you," Matthews said.

"It has been a long time since we last saw each other, Fisher Matthews."

"Yes, it has," Matthews replied.

"These are . . . your new friends? I do not recognize them from my last visit."

"This is Hartinger, Vasquez, and Shephard," Matthews said.

Amitiel slowly nodded her head to each of them in turn. Alex tried to look her in the eye but found that he couldn't. The sight of an alien speaking in English, one who looked so much like the Seraphim, was almost too much to bear.

"I know you must be afraid," she said to them. "We were, as well, when the Seraphim first came to our world."

This caught Alex's attention. "They attacked you, also?" he asked.

Amitiel turned to him with her eerie blank eyes. "They did. We were able to repel them with the force of our armies, but only at great cost to our planet's resources. Particularly our water."

The humans looked at each other.

"What happened to your water?" Matthews asked.

"The Seraphim attacked us in many ways. They are a creative race, and unfortunately this extends to their cruelty. They poisoned our water. Almost all of it."

"On the whole *planet*?" Alex asked, stunned.

Amitiel looked at him again with that expressionless face. "Yes. The whole planet."

"My God," Hartinger said.

"I do not, however, believe they intend to do the same here."

"Why not?"

"Because they have already captured most of you. There would be no need."

Alex frowned. Her logic was chilling.

Matthews cleared his throat. "Amitiel, I have to ask. Why did you come to Earth? Are you here to help us?"

Amitiel bowed her head and was silent for a moment. Then she looked up and said, "I wish I could say that our reason for coming is to lend you aid, Fisher Matthews, but I cannot."

Alex almost unconsciously brought his hand to the gun at his hip.

"You're going to help the Seraphim, then?" Hartinger said. "Help them enslave us?"

Amitiel turned her white eyes on him. "No, friend Hartinger. We will never lend aid to the Seraphim."

"Then why *are* you here?"

Again, Amitiel was silent for a while, as though contemplating her next words. Then, at last, she said, "There has been much discussion among my people whether it was our right to deliver certain knowledge to you. Ultimately, it was decided the time has come. That is part of why I am here. I wished to talk to you again, Fisher Matthews, and tell you the truth."

"And what truth would that be?" Matthews asked.

"The truth of mankind's origin," she answered.

Time seemed to stop suddenly for Alex, and he felt a hollowness in his chest. The words coming out of the alien's mouth were disturbing to say the least, but the idea that she knew something about the beginnings of man—something that he did not know—was almost unbearable.

This was not how it was supposed to be. He *knew* the truth of mankind's origin. A seamless blend of the evolution he had learned of in science class and the magnificent guiding hand of God he knew in his heart to be true.

These were the things that made mankind what it was.

Not whatever lies might come from an alien's mouth.

"What could you possibly know about us?" he spat out before thinking.

They all turned to him, Amitiel included. "I know a great deal, friend Shephard," she said.

"I'm not your *friend.*"

"Shephard," Matthews said, putting a hand up. "Chill."

"You do not trust me," Amitiel said. "This I understand. But I promise you this: what I tell you is the absolute truth, and will give you an answer as to why the Seraphim have been attacking you."

"All right," Matthews said. "Let's hear it."

Amitiel took a moment and looked at each one of them. Then she spoke. "Many millions of years ago, the Seraphim were like you humans, both in mind and body. They looked as you do now, smaller and more fragile.

"But slowly, over time, they evolved into something greater. Something . . . more than human. Their intellect and capabilities of invention knew few boundaries. And though their lifespan grew to many hundreds of years, it was not enough for them. They wished for even longer lives and believed such a thing could be achieved by merging their bodies with the technologies they had created."

"Their bionics," Matthews said.

"Yes. When the first of them became cybernetic, they discovered they could indeed extend their lives by three or four times their natural span. But it was still not enough to satisfy them, and so they continued.

Generation after generation, for thousands of years, they continued to incorporate more and more technology into their natural bodies. But this led to an outcome they did not expect."

"What kind of outcome?" Matthews asked.

"Their bodies became completely dependent upon the technology."

"You mean they can't survive without their bio-tech?" Hartinger said.

"That is correct, friend Hartinger. It is as vital to them as your organs are to you."

"You still haven't explained why they're here," Vasquez said.

"Or why they need our blood," Alex added.

"But I shall," Amitiel said, "in a moment. There is more to the story of the Seraphim, and this will explain all."

Alex cracked the knuckles of his fingers with his thumb. He didn't like this. Amitiel was lecturing to them about the history of the Seraphim as though it were a story told by a campfire. Was she holding them here for some reason? Stalling?

She went on. "After many thousands of years, the Seraphim realized they had made a grave error. Their bodies had become too dependent on their technological interfaces and thus began to break down. They grew sick. Weak. And that is when they came to us."

"I don't understand," Matthews said. "Were they aware of your species earlier?"

"Of course. They created us."

The humans just stared at her.

"They *created* you?"

"The Seraphim are our genetic ancestors. They took their genetic material and nourished it on our home planet, so that we would eventually grow to be like them. In a way, we *are* Seraphim. Just a less evolved version."

Alex thought this made sense. It also explained why they looked so much like the Seraphim.

"The Seraphim, realizing their species was dying, came up with a plan to save themselves. They would take our cells and use the genetic information therein to create new cells for their own bodies, replenishing themselves, working in conjunction with their biotechnology."

"Did you agree to this?" Matthews asked.

"We did not." Amitiel looked away for a moment and did not speak.

"Amitiel? Are you all right?"

"Forgive me, Fisher Matthews. This was a dark time in our past, and I do not enjoy imagining my species as so vulnerable."

"Yeah, tell me what that's like," Vasquez scoffed.

"The Seraphim waited until we were at a point in our evolution that they deemed our cells . . . worthy of being harvested. They told us they didn't want cells that were too primitive, and so they were patient. But their patience was their undoing, as it turned out."

"How's that?" Matthews asked.

"Because they allowed us to evolve. We became capable of matching their technology with technology that could repel them. By the time they came to us with the intent of harvesting our bodies, we were ready to fight back. There were many battles, and my people came to call this time the Harvest War. It was during this time that our natural resources were decimated, and our usable water became scarce."

"This was thousands of years ago?"

"Hundreds of thousands."

"How have you survived?"

"There is a small moon that orbits our planet. This moon contained water so we were forced to move as many survivors as possible. However, this transition presented its own difficulties and we suffered additional casualties. We don't want to see this same fate fall upon the humans."

"What happened to the Seraphim after you fought them off?" Matthew asked.

Amitiel looked away for a moment in what Alex realized was a common response for her. She didn't seem to show much urgency in providing intel, that was for sure. "They regrouped," she said after a minute. "They realized their error in waiting for us to evolve past a certain point. So they decided to try again."

At this, Alex felt his heart skip a beat. Something didn't feel right.

A memory suddenly sprang to the forefront of his thoughts: he was four years old, and his mother was telling him about how God created man in his image. He remembered how at peace that had made him feel at the time.

And even though as he became older his views shifted more toward a theistic evolution; the idea that God's hand had led man to where he was today was the foundation of his belief. It was part of him, down to his very core.

"What do you mean, 'try again?'" he said suddenly. His voice was harsh.

"After we proved to be a failed experiment," Amitiel said, "the Seraphim traveled farther away from their home planet, looking for yet another world that could sustain life in the same way as theirs."

Alex's hands curled into tight fists, squeezing so fiercely he felt his nails pierce the soft flesh of his palm. "No . . ." he whispered.

"Eventually they found it. And they called it Earth."

"No!" Alex shouted.

"Shephard, calm down," Hartinger said.

"She's lying!"

"I assure you, friend Shephard, I am not." Amitiel gazed at him with that blank, white-eyed stare.

"This is bullshit! Why are we listening to this?"

"Yo, let's just hear her out, man," Vasquez said.

"You're lying," Alex said, staring right back into the void of Amitiel's eyes.

"Why do you say this?" she asked.

"Because we know how we evolved. Some of the early primates evolved into hominids, which eventually became us. This has been proven over and over again by our top scientists. Are you trying to tell us that didn't happen?"

"Life on this planet evolved as you understand it, yes. But it did not happen as randomly as your science would lead you to believe. All of your evolution occurred under the direction of the Seraphim."

That was it. Those were the words Alex somehow knew, somehow dreaded, she was going to say. He turned away from the rest of them, staggering down the hall. He thought for a moment he might pass out, and then with greater urgency knew he was going to vomit. He rushed for the exit, bashed open the door with his shoulder, and fell to his knees, emptying his guts on the dusty road.

Everything was spinning. He didn't know what to, how to make it stop. Everything he believed, everything he knew in his heart to be real, was a sick, perverted lie. It was all the Seraphim. Always.

And if the Seraphim created them . . . did that mean there was no God? He threw up again.

"Jesus. Shephard, you okay?" Vasquez's voice came from behind him.

He was vaguely aware of her kneeling next to him, of her hand on his back. But it felt like it was happening to another person. He didn't feel like he was in his own body. "No," he croaked.

"Listen, man. I know that's a lot to hear. But she's not done telling us things, and we got to know this intel."

Alex spat, trying to get the sour taste out of his mouth. He turned to look at Vasquez out of the corner of his eye. "How are you so calm?" he asked. "We just found out we were a fucking science experiment."

"This is about God, right?"

Alex looked away.

Vasquez gently ruffled his hair. "I'm not like you, Shephard. I never had any faith to begin with. Doesn't hurt so bad when there's no foundation to break. But I get it. For you, this is probably about the worst thing you could hear."

Alex thought he might vomit again but fought it off.

"Come on," she said. She hooked an arm under his, helping him to his feet. "Time to man up."

"I can't go back in there."

"Sure you can. You're a marine."

Alex nodded, spit one more time, and followed her back inside.

He glared at Amitiel as he entered. Hartinger and Matthews looked worried. "You all right, Shephard?" Matthews asked.

"Affirmative, sir," Alex said.

He crossed his arms against his chest.

"I am sorry if this information causes you pain," Amitiel said.

"I bet," Alex muttered under his breath.

"Please continue, Amitiel," Matthews said. "You said that humanity began because the Seraphim manipulated our evolution."

"That is correct, Fisher Matthews. The reason was twofold. First, the Seraphim wished to create a younger, less advanced version of themselves that would not be able to fight them off. But beyond that, they needed cells that had no synthetic integration, and we had already begun performing this process, though not to the extent of the Seraphim. We are their failed experiment. But you are their success."

Matthews said, "And that's why they're taking our blood. And why our blood is compatible with their own."

"Yes."

"This is all . . . very disturbing, as I'm sure you can imagine, Amitiel."

"Yes. I understand, Fisher Matthews. And though it pains me to say this, I'm afraid that is not the end of what I must tell you."

The four humans all glanced at each other. Vasquez, Hartinger, and Matthews all seemed specifically worried about Alex. This wasn't a conversation that was pleasant for anybody.

"This concerns the other reason why the Malakhim have come to Earth," Amitiel said, her voice somber.

"Which is?" Matthews asked.

"As I said, the water on our planet was ruined, and we, like you, require water to survive. We are here for yours."

"*What?*" Vasquez burst out.

"Across your planet, our ships have begun collecting water, draining your lakes and rivers."

"I don't understand," Matthews said. "I thought you said your moon provided you water. What exactly is your plan?"

"Our moon is very small in comparison to our planet. We have taken all that the moon can provide. And now we have come for Earth's water."

"What—*all* of it?"

"Most of your fresh water. As I said, almost all of ours was poisoned, and is now unusable."

"Amitiel," Matthews said. "You can't just . . . you can't just come and *take* our water. You'll kill us."

Amitiel was silent again for an infuriating amount of time. Then she spoke. "It was agreed upon by our councils that your world . . . your species . . . is already lost. The Seraphim have claimed you. The damage has already been done. And since we are desperately in need of water, we must take this opportunity."

"What?" Vasquez said.

Suddenly Alex seemed to lose it. "You fucking alien bitch!" he shouted, unholstering his sidearm.

"Whoa!" Hartinger shouted. "Shephard, back down."

"Back down?" Shephard said. "Are you kidding me? They're just as bad as the Seraphim!"

"For what it is worth," Amitiel said, "I am in agreement. I do not think what we are doing here is right. Many of my people do not. But it was decided by our councils. And their word is law."

Her words stopped Alex in his tracks. It didn't occur to him that there might be dissension within the alien race.

"These councils," Alex said, "that's your government?"

"Yes," Amitiel said.

"Can't they be persuaded to find another solution?"

"I am sorry to say their decision is absolute. It weighs on me, as I firmly believe our reason for being here is wrong. But I must obey."

Matthews approached Amitiel. "Is there anything else? Anything more we should know?"

"No, Fisher Matthews. That is all I have to say. Except . . . I am so sorry. Please forgive me."

"I know it's not your decision, Amitiel."

Amitiel bowed her head and moved away, and Matthews turned to the rest of them. "Let's roll out," he said.

2109

"You're telling me all of mankind was an experiment?" the younger man asked. His eyes were wide, his expression raw.

The old man looked down at his empty glass. "I know it's not an easy truth to hear."

"Not easy? All our questions . . . why we're here, what's the meaning of life . . . and the answer is we were bred for fucking spare parts?"

The old man nodded, and the younger man stood up. He moved out into the garden, crossed his arms, and looked up at the sky.

"Would you rather I sugarcoat it for you?" the old man asked.

"Don't patronize me."

"I'm not. Or at least, I didn't mean to. Sometimes my words come out wrong. I'm quite old."

The younger man balled his hands into fists, released them, and then balled them up again. "I just can't believe it."

"Well," the old man said, "it's not an easy pill to swallow for any living creature. But it is, unfortunately, the truth."

"All these years . . . all this time that's passed since the Harvest War . . . why has nobody talked about this?"

"Why would they?"

The younger man spun around furiously. "Because it seems kind of fucking important, don't you think?"

"Is it?" The old man sighed. "Whether we were put here by a loving God's design or the machinations of an alien race, the fact remains that we are here. That isn't changed by the details of our origin."

"A lot of people will be up in arms about this claim."

"It's not a claim. It's what happened."

"They'll say it's a lie."

"Let them. Or, if you like, leave this part out of your report. After all, you're performing the interview. The narrative is yours to control."

The younger man turned his head away from the old man and toward the koi swimming in the little pond. He walked over to a small box, opened it, and scooped out a handful of brown pellets. He scattered them into the water, and the koi hungrily swam to the surface, attacking the pellets.

"Why did you just do that?" the old man asked.

"What? Feed the fish? Well, they'd starve if I didn't."

"But why right now?"

"I don't know," the younger man snapped. "I guess I find it soothing."

"That they depend on you?"

"Maybe."

"Would you say it's your will to dominate them?"

"What? Of course not."

"You wish to provide for them, without dominating them. Well, maybe that's how the Seraphim thought of us," the old man said.

The younger man shook his head. "But I'm not ripping them apart and taking their blood."

The old man leaned back in his chair and folded his hands on his lap. "But if your survival depended on it, or the survival of the human race . . . if you needed their blood to stay alive . . . you'd take it, wouldn't you?"

The younger man looked away.

CHAPTER 8

O n the ride back to Fort Hood Alex was silent.
Vasquez, Hartinger, and Matthews didn't have
much to say either. Alex wondered if they were
thinking the same thoughts as he was. Terribly dark,
utterly nihilistic thoughts.

If humanity was the result of genetic tinkering by
the Seraphim, then everything really was a lie. God.
Jesus. The Garden of Eden. The Crucifixion and the
Resurrection.

Lies, all of it.

Humans weren't the blessed children of God. They
were just *things,* created in a lab by monsters.

And if mankind was so insignificant . . . did he
really even have a soul? He felt a wave of nausea hit him,
but there was nothing left in his stomach to throw up.

When they returned to the base, he told the others
he was going to stay outside for a bit.

"You sure, man?" Vasquez said. "Maybe you
shouldn't be alone."

"I just need some air," he replied.

Vasquez's brow furrowed.

"I'm fine," Alex said.

"Yeah. Okay," Vasquez said, looking unconvinced. She followed Hartinger and Matthews inside.

Alex sat on a bench on the outside perimeter of the fort. He thought he might cry, but no tears came. His anguish had turned into something different, something worse.

Emptiness.

He felt nothing. How, after all, could he feel sad or hurt or lost if there was no soul inside of him? How could anyone have ever felt anything? Was it all just an illusion? Did the Seraphim place the lie of emotions within them? Did they *breed* it into them?

Without his even realizing it, Alex's hand had gone to his chest, fingering the cross that lay beneath his shirt, as he always did when facing a crisis of conscience.

So stupid, he thought.

He reached into his shirt and grasped the cross in his hand. With one hard pull, he broke the clasp of the chain, and the cross came loose. He looked at it for a moment. Many people wore crosses, but so rarely did they ever truly look at them. He always tried to really look at his cross, to make himself remember what it meant to him: that Jesus suffered for days, that he endured the worst agony a human being could possibly endure, and that he did it all so that there would be less suffering for the rest of us. All his life, that knowledge had brought Alex such a transcendent feeling of peace, of being loved and cared for and protected. That there was someone out there who would never leave him.

And now it turned out, this was all a lie. He reared his arm back and threw the cross as far as he could, not looking to see where it landed.

He wasn't sure how long he sat out there alone, but soon he sensed a presence behind him, and without turning, he knew who it was. "Hey," he said.

"Hey," Kate answered, her voice barely more than a whisper. She sat next to him on the bench. From where they sat, they could see a small field bordered by a stretch of trees. Alex was amazed by how peaceful it looked, like the field and the trees themselves were utterly unaware of the horror that had visited their world.

"Natalia told me what happened," Kate said.

"Everything?"

"Yeah, everything."

"That Vasquez. Always did have a big mouth."

Kate slid her hand into his and intertwined their fingers. "Let's go for a walk."

"It might not be safe."

"We'll stick close to the entrance," she said. "Come on."

Reluctantly, he let her pull him up to his feet. She wrapped an arm around his waist, and he placed his arm around her shoulder. Together, they walked down the path that led to the parking lot, surrounded by tiny trees. It would have been peaceful had Alex not felt like his guts were turning inside out.

"You believe what the alien said?" Kate asked.

"She had no reason to lie about it."

"No . . . I guess she didn't." Kate let out a deep sigh. "I wonder if it was just as hard for them."

"Who?"

"The Malakhim. I wonder if they thought they were the center of the universe, maybe the only intelligent species out there. Maybe they prayed to God every night, the God who created them, just like we do. And then they found out what we just found out."

Alex frowned. "I hadn't really thought about it. When we were talking to her, she seemed more like a robot than a living thing. Hard to imagine them having *feelings*."

"Still. I wonder."

Alex leaned his cheek onto the top of Kate's head and squeezed her close. "You always look for the good in everybody, babe. Even aliens. That's probably the biggest reason I love you so damn much."

Kate squeezed him back. "I love you, too. And, well, I know I haven't really had any time to process this, but I've been thinking. Thinking about what it means if the Seraphim really did make us."

Alex looked down at her, his eyebrows raised.

She went on. "I mean, if you stop and think about it, it's not really all that different from what you and I believed before."

"How can you say that?"

"Well, we always listened to what the science tells us about evolution and natural selection. And we never had a problem incorporating those ideas into our faith, you know? Sure, we evolved from hominids, which evolved from the early mammals, and on and on. But this evolution occurred because that was God's plan."

"Only now we know it wasn't," Alex said, his words bitter and taut. "It wasn't God's plan at all. It was *theirs.*"

"But that's just it," Kate said. "We got some new information on where we came from. The Seraphim manipulated things so humanity would eventually appear in our current phase as a result of evolution, right?"

"According to the Malakhim, yeah."

"So how is that any different than evolution being moved in a different direction by a volcano erupting, or a meteor hitting the earth?"

"What are you saying?"

Kate stopped walking and looked him in the eye. She clasped his face with both hands. "I still have faith. I think maybe, just maybe, the Seraphim making us was part of God's plan. Maybe they were just the method that he used in order to get us here."

Alex thought for a minute. Though he wanted to protest, there was something about what she was saying that made so much sense. "My lord," he said. "You really are the smartest person I've ever met."

"And don't you forget it," she said. She stood up on her tiptoes and kissed him. He embraced her, breathing in the scent of her hair, feeling the warmth of her small body. His hand traveled to her belly, and she covered his hand with hers.

"We don't have any reason to give up on God," Kate said. "I know it feels like he's given up on us, but I think it's just a test. Like how Joseph or Abraham were tested. But we have to hang on to our faith, because it'll help us win this thing. And then it'll make the world better for our baby."

Alex pressed his mouth against hers. He felt overcome with love for this strong, brilliant woman he was lucky enough to call his. "Marry me," he said.

"What?" She looked at him like he'd lost his mind.

"Before the world went to hell, I was saving up for a ring. Never did manage to buy it before . . . all this." He dropped to one knee and looked up at her. "And I doubt I could find a ring now, so . . . Kate, will you marry me?"

She laughed even as her eyes brimmed with tears. She nodded vigorously, and then squeaked out, "Yes, I will."

Alex rose and kissed her once again, and held her close. "Just imagine I put a really expensive-looking ring on your finger," he whispered.

"Roger that, Corporal," she whispered back.

* * *

Alex slept on and off that night, his arms wrapped around Kate, who nestled into his shoulder. When he did nod off, he dreamed of Amitiel, of the hideous sight of an alien speaking a language he could understand.

He woke up shivering each time.

When morning finally came, Kate yawned and blinked a few times, then turned to him and smiled. "Morning, my betrothed," she said.

He chuckled. "Betrothed, huh?"

"It's a good word."

He kissed her, and then stretched. He got out of bed and began dressing. "We should get down to the mess hall."

"Yes, please, I'm starving," Kate said. "Then again, I'm always starving now."

Alex turned to her. "Yeah?"

"Yeah," Kate said. She rubbed her belly with one hand. "Eating for two. You know how it goes."

Alex smiled and embraced her. "We're going to bring this baby into a good world," he said. "Somehow. And when we do . . . it won't be like this. I promise."

Kate looked up at him. "I believe you."

When they'd finished dressing, they exited their quarters and were heading towards the mess hall when Vasquez rounded the corner. "Hey, Shephard, I was just coming to find you," she said.

"What's up?"

"Conners says we received a radio signal from some human survivors. An SOS. There's civilians out there. On their own."

"Oh, my God," Kate said. "Where?"

"Just over the state line, I think he said. Come on, Shephard. We gotta save 'em."

Alex looked at Kate, who bit her lip. Then, after a moment, she looked at him and simply said, "Go."

"Are you sure?"

"They're human. That means we've got to help them, if we can. I'll be all right."

Alex kissed her, and then followed Vasquez down the corridor.

"Think of it, man," Vasquez said. "Civilians out there alone all this time. How do you think they survived?"

"Must have laid low," Alex said.

"Yeah, must have," Vasquez said, nodding. "Gotta live like moles to avoid the Seraphim's sensors. Whoever they are, they gotta be some ballsy-ass people."

"Good. We could use all the ballsy-ass people we can get."

Vasquez laughed. "Truth."

They arrived at Conners' office to find Matthews and Hartinger waiting for them, along with the Sergeant Major and Richie, the private who'd greeted them with a gun when they first came to the Fort. Conners was in the middle of a sentence when he looked over, eyebrows arched, towards Alex and Vasquez. "Ah, the marines have arrived. Shephard, Vasquez, thanks for joining us."

"We got a distress beacon from civilians?" Alex asked. Technically, he shouldn't have spoken in a debriefing until being asked a question, but he figured there was no reason to stand on formality, even if Conners did seem committed to it.

Conners lips twitched, but he didn't scold Alex. "That's right. Just across the state border, in New Mexico. Since the four of you have had the most success dealing with outside travel, I'd like you to go round up these friendlies. Private Pratt here, as it happens, is from a town not far from where the radio signal came from, so he's going to act as your guide."

"Don't tell me," Vasquez said. "Roswell."

Everyone in the room laughed, including Alex. It was the first time he remembered laughing in some time.

"No," Richie said. "A place called Dayton, off the 285. I'm from Lake Arthur, just a half hour north. But my high school girlfriend lived in Dayton. I know the area."

"How long ago was high school for you?" Alex asked. Richie looked like a kid.

"I graduated last year, sir," Richie said.

God damn, Alex thought. He'd at least had four years of college before going military. Richie really *was* a kid. "You sure you want to come, Richie? I'm sure we can find the friendlies without you."

"We don't know what we might encounter out there, sir," Richie said. "And I'm familiar with the land-scape, so I know all the places to hide. My girlfriend and I got pretty good at finding – you know – places to not get caught."

There was another round of appreciative laughter, and then all faces turned serious. "You leave in an hour, people," Conners said. "Dismissed."

* * *

The crew of two marines, two CIA sleeper agents, and an army private piled into a jeep in the main hangar area of the base beneath Fort Hood. Richie was in the driver's seat, and with confidence he pulled out of the hangar and into a long corridor that gradually led up to surface level. When they neared the exit, it looked like the corridor ended with a dead stop, disappearing up to the ceiling.

This must be the surface, Alex thought.

About a hundred yards before the end, Richie pulled to a stop next to a panel on the wall. He punched in a few buttons, and a panel on the ceiling opened up, allowing them to drive up the rest of the ramp and into the open air. The tunnel had led them onto a grassy field a half mile away from Fort Hood, and Alex was reminded of the tunnel they had taken out of Camp Lejeune, urged on by Master Sergeant Brady, right after the camp fell to the Seraphim. It felt like it had happened a lifetime ago.

Alex gritted his teeth.

A lifetime ago. It really was a lifetime ago for Hoffman and Chan. Literally.

He shook his head sadly.

Next to him, Vasquez looked over at him and cocked her head. "You okay?" she asked.

"Yeah," he said, looking out the window.

"Still thinking about what the alien said? The Malakhim?"

Alex couldn't help but laugh. It seemed that there was no shortage of horrors to brood over. "Nope," he said. "Something else."

Vasquez nodded, but didn't pry any further. "Yeah, I guess there's going to be a lot more 'something else's' before this is over."

"Roger that."

They fell into a silence, which was soon broken by Richie. "Up ahead's the Interstate," he said. "It's the fastest route to Dayton. Only problem is a lot of attacks seem to happen on big open roads. What do you think?"

"The scenic route—would it provide more cover?" Hartinger asked.

"Not really, sir," Richie said. "There's not a lot of dense tree cover around here. Pretty much anywhere we go, we'll be visible by air."

"Fucking fantastic," Hartinger said. "Then I vote for speed. Matthews?"

"Sounds like a plan," Matthews said.

"Interstate it is, then," Richie said. He pulled onto the large road and gunned the engine.

The scenery flew by them as Richie tore down the Interstate at almost one hundred miles per hour. Alex appreciated the young private's need for speed. With no one else on the road, it wasn't like they were likely to get into a collision, and the less time they spent exposed the better.

"So, Richie, you grew up around here, huh?" Matthews said.

"Affirmative, sir," Richie replied. "Haven't been back since I enlisted, though."

"How come?"

Richie was silent for a moment. Then he said, "I didn't get along that well with my parents, sir. They were lifelong church folk, and pacifists. They didn't approve of anything military."

"What made you want to sign up?"

"My uncle was in the Army. He got killed in Afghanistan when he was just two weeks out from being done with his last tour. He and his men were training Afghan army members in an area they thought was clear of any Taliban presence. They were wrong."

"What happened?" Hartinger asked.

"They took some mortar fire, a few rounds. And that was it, the Taliban guys turned tail and ran like the pussies they are. My uncle was hit in the first wave. There wasn't even enough left of him to send back to bury."

"Ah, fuck," Vasquez whispered.

"So," Richie said, "that was the spring of last year, my senior year. I'd been accepted to the community college, was going to get my associate's degree, and then maybe get a bachelor's in something. But my uncle, man . . . he was my best friend. My hero growing up, you know? And knowing what happened to him . . . I couldn't just keep going like nothing happened. New Mexico might not be the nicest place in the world, but it's fucking paradise compared to the Middle East. And he chose to go there to protect my right to live free. What kind of man would I be if I didn't do the same?"

There was a moment of quiet, then Richie said, "I didn't mean that to be sexist. I should have said 'what kind of person.'"

"Hah!" Vasquez said. "No offense taken. Besides, I'm way more of a man than Shephard here."

"You fucking wish," Alex said, smirking.

They all chuckled as they flew down the road. Alex caught a quick glimpse of the sign showing the exit for Dayton.

As Richie pulled onto the exit ramp, he went on, saying, "I figured I'd be in Afghanistan or Iraq by now, continuing my uncle's mission. Never expected I'd be part of the first war mankind ever waged against extra-motherfuckin'-terrestrials."

Vasquez grinned. "Kind of puts the Taliban in perspective, huh?"

"I'll say," Richie agreed. "In fact—" He never finished his sentence.

The road on Alex's side of the vehicle exploded in an eruption of dirt and pavement, and a deafening shockwave resounded through the air. The jeep flipped over on its side before any of them had time to cry out. It rolled completely over onto the roof so that all five of them dangled precariously, suspended only by their seat belts. Alex realized he was holding his breath, so he sucked in air and felt a harsh ache in his torso. It was possible he'd bruised or even broken a rib. He looked over and saw Vasquez and Matthews hanging upside down next to him. Both were conscious, but blinking, confused.

"We're hit!" Alex said. "We're under attack!"

He struggled to unlock his seat belt as he heard the sound of gunfire outside. Through his haze, he tried to see if Richie and Hartinger had somehow already exited the vehicle and were returning fire, but they were hanging in the front of the vehicle. Hartinger was trying to undo his seat belt with one hand while the other braced against the ceiling of the car, now underneath them.

Richie looked to be knocked out cold, and a gash was dripping blood from his temple.

"Fuck . . ." Vasquez moaned. "Who's firing?"

"I don't know," Alex said. He finally managed to undo the belt, and gravity took hold of him, yanking him down against the car's ceiling. He felt the bones in his neck crunch on impact, but this was just a momentary pain. Somehow he'd mostly gotten through the car flipping uninjured. He pressed his hand against what was now the floor and immediately regretted it. Thousands of tiny shards of broken glass bit at his fingers. He yanked his hand away, and blood leaked from his palm.

There was more gunfire outside. "What the fuck is happening out there?" he asked.

"I don't know! I can't see," Hartinger said as he struggled with his own belt. Matthews and Vasquez also tugged at their bindings, but Richie only moaned, barely stirring.

Struggling, Alex righted himself and pushed his body through the pain to grasp onto the door handle. He realized right away it wouldn't open, for it was bent and crushed at impossible angles. He brought his foot forward and kicked through the glass, and could hear Matthews doing the same behind him. At last, he was able to drag his body out onto the pavement, and immediately felt two rough hands hook under his armpits.

"Be careful now, boy," a gruff voice said. "They're gone. We chased 'em away. But those injuries look mighty nasty."

Alex looked up and squinted. The sun blazed right into his eyes, and the man helping him was standing in front of it, casting his body in silhouette.

"What happened?" Alex rasped. He could hear the sound of the others struggling to get free of the jeep.

"Some of them damn aliens shot at you with their laser beams," the man responded. "I was out here with my wife and son, looking for supplies. Good thing we came along when we did. We always have our guns with us. Never know what you might find when going out salvaging."

Alex's eyes adjusted slowly to the bright light, and he was able to make out the man's features. He was around fifty, with tan leathery skin and deep-set lines around his eyes and mouth. He had wispy dark gray hair and salt-and-pepper stubble on his chin, and he wore simple work pants and a torn T-shirt. He would have looked like an extra from a comedy starring Walter Matthau were it not for the AK-47 slung over his back and the hunting dagger hanging from his belt.

"Some help over here, Pa!" a male voice came from the other side of the jeep, and the man took off. Alex pulled himself off the ground and shakily got to his feet. He saw a woman about the same age as the man. She was struggling to help the bearded man pull Hartinger out the hole in the window that the agent had created. Alex moved to help her, and together they were able to extract Hartinger from the vehicle.

"Thank you, ma'am," Hartinger said, cradling his shoulder.

"Don't thank us yet," the woman said. "We're still sitting ducks out here. Who knows when those things'll be back? We got to get inside."

"You'll get no argument from me," Hartinger said. "Shephard, Richie's hurt. See if you can help him."

"It's okay, we got him!" came Vasquez's voice from the other side of the jeep. Alex moved around the vehicle and saw the man who helped him standing next to a younger man about Richie's age. He looked enough like the older man that Alex was certain he was his son.

Vasquez and Matthews were lifting a barely conscious Richie off the ground.

"Our van's big enough for all of us," the older man said. "Come on. Ain't no time to waste."

He turned and marched quickly to the side of the road towards an ancient-looking van. As he jumped behind the wheel, the younger man pulled open the side door, and the rest of the group got inside. A minute later, they were speeding down the Interstate.

"My name's Ann," the woman said, running her fingers through her dirty hair. "That's my husband at the wheel, Michael, and our boy, Joseph."

"My name's Hartinger," Hartinger said. "This is Shephard, Vasquez, Matthews, and Pratt."

"Y'all ain't got any first names?"

"Sorry," Hartinger said. "Military. You know how it goes. My name's Kevin, and this is Alex, Natalia, Fisher, and Richie."

"Military," Michael said from the front of the van. "Don't suppose y'all were answering our distress call?"

Alex perked up. "You were the ones who sent out the call?"

"Yes, sir, we sure are. We didn't think anyone would answer it, but we had to try."

"Are there more of you from where you came from?" the son, Joseph, asked.

"Yeah," Alex said. "We've got a whole base full of both military and civilians at Fort Hood over in Texas."

"Really?" Joseph said. His face brightened considerably.

"Don't get too excited now, Joseph," Michael snapped. "Fort Hood's a far drive. These folks are military, and *we* had to end up rescuing *them*. We'd never survive traveling that far."

Alex looked over and saw Hartinger frown, and realized he was doing the same thing.

"It's a dangerous trip, for damn sure," Hartinger said. "But Shephard and Vasquez here drove all around the damn country before finally ending up at Fort Hood."

"Yeah?" Michael said. "How many did you lose on the way?"

Shame burned suddenly in Alex's chest. "Two," he said quietly.

"And y'all got combat training," Michael said. "How do we know we can get there safely?"

"Unfortunately, there are no guarantees anymore, sir," Alex said. "Not since, you know, the apocalypse happened and all. But I can sure as hell promise you we'll do everything we can to keep you and your family safe."

"Let's just get back to our home first," Ann said. "Then we can discuss how we'll make the trip. I've got a big stew going; should be piping hot when we get there."

Alex looked at his companions. After the military rations they'd been eating since getting to Fort Hood, a homemade stew sounded like the most amazing thing he'd ever heard of.

* * *

Alex brought the spoon up to his mouth and blew on it, waiting for the stew to cool. But then his impatience got the better of him, and he shoved the spoon into his mouth and swallowed it all. It burned the roof of his mouth, but he didn't care. The taste of pork, vegetables, and broth was the most comforting sensation he'd had since this whole adventure started. By the looks of his friends digging into the stew around him, they were all having the same experience. He felt bad that Richie, resting in one of the bedrooms, had to miss out on this.

"Amazing, ma'am," he said. "Absolutely delicious."

"Well, I'm glad you like it, son," Ann said. "Benefits of living on a pig farm. We're well stocked with meat. For the time being, at least."

"Aren't you going to have any?" Matthews asked. Their new hosts had waited on them, but hadn't taken any bowls for themselves.

"We ate right before we left the house," Ann said. "We still need to build up an appetite."

"You folks have been out here all on your own this whole time?" Vasquez asked.

"Yes, ma'am," Michael said. "We haven't seen too many of them flyers, not out here. We stay indoors as much as we can. Lucky for you we were out scavenging when they attacked y'all."

"Hey, can I ask you a question?" Joseph, the son, said to Vasquez. He was staring at her in a funny way.

"Sure, kid," Vasquez said. "What's up?"

"How come you shaved your head like that?"

"Joseph!" Ann said, smacking her son on the back of his head. "Don't be rude. Ain't a proper thing to ask a lady you don't know."

"No, it's okay, ma'am," Vasquez said. She looked at Joseph. "I shaved my head because I'm a marine. Women don't technically have to do it, but the men do, and I don't much care for special treatment. After I shaved it I realized it was pretty damn practical for those of us who live a . . . well, an action-packed life. So I keep it shaved."

Joseph shrugged. "I think it'd look more pretty if it was long."

"Joseph!" Ann yelled at her son again.

Vasquez laughed. "Don't worry about it, ma'am," she said. "That's not the first time I heard that."

"Joseph, go to the barn and tend to the pigs," Michael said.

"Yes, Pa," Joseph said, and quickly exited the room.

Michael sighed. "Sorry about him," he said. "He's a bit simple. He didn't get a chance to talk to many people 'sides us even before the aliens came."

"I'm sorry to hear that, sir," Vasquez said.

Hartinger brought a spoonful of stew to his mouth and winced, dropping his spoon and clutching his shoulder.

"You all right?" Michael asked.

"Not sure," Hartinger said, wincing again. "I might have broken something in the crash. It can wait until we get back to the base. Our medical staff—"

"Son, if you're hurt, we gotta tend to ya," Michael said. "We've got a medical kit out in the garage. Why don't you come with me?"

Hartinger thought for a moment, then nodded. "Much obliged, sir," he said, and stood, though Alex noticed it was with great effort. He seemed shaky on his feet as he followed Michael out the door.

Something bothered Alex, though he couldn't put his finger on it. He had been feeling a dull pain in the back of his head for the past few minutes, which he had written off as a result of the jeep flipping and throttling his body, but he also felt hot. Sick. Something was wrong. He looked around at his companions, and everyone seemed to be sagging a bit in their chair. For a moment, the most paranoid part of Alex's brain wondered if the Seraphim might be using some sort of sonic weapon, operating on a frequency they couldn't hear. But then he looked up at Ann, who walked to and from the table, completely unaffected.

It was then he realized he only began to feel sick after he ate her stew.

His vision began to cloud, and the last thing he saw before he passed out was Ann standing there, watching them with her hands on her hips, saying, "Sure took ya long enough."

* * *

"Shephard?"

Alex heard the voice, but it sounded like it was coming through a heavy blanket.

"Shephard. You got to wake up, buddy."

The voice sounded clearer now. More defined.

Matthew's, Alex thought.

"Open your eyes, Shephard."

He hadn't realized his eyes were closed. Slowly, he opened them. The first thing he noticed was the room was dark. The second thing he noticed was that it stank of human waste.

"Where the fuck are we?"

"Those motherfuckers roofied us and locked us up. The bitch must have put the drugs in the stew." It was Vasquez. Alex turned to his left and was just able to make out her form. His eyes struggled to adjust to the dim lighting.

"What?" he asked. He looked down and saw his wrists were shackled with large, crude iron cuffs. They looked homemade. "Why?"

"We're offerings," a voice Alex didn't recognize said from the darkness. It was a woman.

"Who said that?"

"My name's Rachel," the woman said. "I was a farmhand for the Johnsons. That's the family that's holding us here."

Alex looked around desperately. His vision had adjusted now, and he saw there were five other people in the room with them, in addition to his crew. They were all shackled with the rough iron manacles, which in turn were bound with a long chain to a pipe that ran across the bottom of one of the walls.

Alex struggled against his bonds. "Why the fuck are they doing this? What do you mean we're offerings?"

"To save their own skin," Rachel said, looking Alex dead in the eye, "they're going to give us to the aliens."

CHAPTER 9

"**W**hat?" Alex said. "Are you fucking kidding me?"

"It's true," another woman said. "I heard them say it. They said they reckon they can keep collecting people by sending out that radio distress signal."

"And as long as they have people to hand over, they figure the aliens will leave 'em be," Rachel said.

"We're their insurance," another prisoner, a man, said.

Vasquez hissed, "Fucking unbelievable."

Immediately, Alex began straining at his cuffs, and Vasquez, Richie, Matthews, and Hartinger all followed suit. Alex pivoted around and pressed his boots against the piping and pulled hard, but the iron manacles weren't going to release any time soon, and he knew it was pointless to cut his wrists up trying.

"They're morons if they think the Seraphim would cut them a deal," Hartinger said. "That's not their M.O."

"Desperate people do stupid fucking things," Matthews said.

"How long have you all been here?" Alex said, looking at the other prisoners.

"Two weeks, for me," Rachel said. "I was the first. Nancy here and the others were captured about a week ago."

The other woman who spoke nodded at the sound of her name.

"Have the Seraphim been here?"

"No, not as far as we can see," Rachel said.

Alex looked at his companions.

"The attack," Richie said. "It must have been them. None of us actually saw any Seraphim, right?"

"Right," Alex said. "They must have rigged the road with explosives. Caught us off guard, and then made up that bullshit about them scaring the Seraphim away. I *knew* something was off about them."

"Fucking lunatics!" Vasquez shouted, projecting her voice as much as she could. "This won't help you!"

There was the sound of footsteps outside the door, and then slowly it creaked open, revealing Michael with Joseph behind him. Michael pushed his son forward and into the room. "Get in there, boy," he said. "Don't be all squirrelly about it. Got to show 'em who's boss."

Joseph walked up to them, clearly nervous but trying to cover it up by throwing on a macho expression. "You keep it down in here," he said. "I . . . I mean it, now."

Hartinger ignored the boy and craned his head toward Michael. "You're a fool if you think this will save your family," he said. "The Seraphim aren't human. They don't cut deals."

Michael shrugged and nodded towards his son. "One of your prisoners is ignoring you, son," he said. "What do you do?"

Joseph swallowed but said nothing.

"Come on, now, boy. Just like with the pigs when they get uppity. What do you do?"

Joseph walked up to Hartinger, squared his shoulders, and backhanded the man across the face. The *crack* of his hand on Hartinger's cheek reverberated throughout the room.

"Show 'im who's boss," Joseph whispered.

"What was that?" Michael asked. "Couldn't hear ya."

"Show 'im who's boss," the boy said, louder.

"Atta boy. That's how we do."

Hartinger glared, not at the young man who had just hit him, but at Michael. He said nothing.

Michael walked into the room then, and addressed them all. "Now, then," he said. "I don't want to hear any more hollering from you all in here. We're trying to have a peaceful dinner. I know none of this is ideal, and I'm sorry the accommodations can't be more to your liking, but I'm afraid this is all we've got to work with."

"Michael," Matthews said, keeping his voice even. "I understand you're trying to protect your family. I do.

But you have to listen to me. I've been studying the Seraphim for almost my entire career. They see themselves as so far superior to humans, we don't even warrant a second thought. They will not negotiate with you, or cut you a deal. When they come for us, they'll take you, your wife, and your son right along with us."

"Maybe they will, maybe they won't," Michael said. "But I got a feeling they'll like what they see when I show 'em how much I can give 'em."

"Don't bet on it," Hartinger said.

Michael looked at the scoffing Hartinger, and then cocked his head curiously. "And just what the hell are *you* doing?"

Alex followed Michael's eye line and saw he was looking at Richie. The young soldier was seated with his arms folded—as much as they could be with the manacles—on his lap.

"What, me? Nothing," Richie said.

"You aiming to get free, huh?" Michael said, stomping over to where Richie was chained to the pipe.

"No, sir," Richie said.

But it was clear he was lying. Michael grabbed his wrists and pulled them up, forcing his manacled arms to straighten. A small bit of copper wire was inserted into the keyhole of one of his cuffs.

He'd been discreetly trying to pick the lock.

"Well, now, ain't this something?" Michael said. "Where'd you get this wire? Ah, hell, it don't really matter, anyhow. Should've maybe expected you all would be a bit rowdier than the others, what with all your military training and all. But I sure as hell didn't think you'd try to escape this damn quick."

"We're human beings, Michael," Matthews said. Alex noticed that was the second time he'd used Michael's name. His mind flashed back to early training about what to do when captured. One of the first things they teach you is to try and form a bond with your captors on a human level. Human beings are hardwired to respond to the sound of their own names. Alex hoped Matthews was successful.

"So?"

"So you can't keep us locked up like animals. Do the right thing, Michael. Let us go. We can offer your family protection at our base."

Michael looked at Matthews, and then back at Richie. "What do you think, kid?" he asked. "Your boss there telling the truth?"

"Of course," Richie said. "We can help you."

"Huh," Michael said.

Without another word, he reached behind him and pulled a small pistol out of the back of his waistband. He then cocked it, took aim, and fired a round right into the middle of Richie's forehead. The boy's head snapped back, and his body slumped to the ground, lifeless.

"No!" Vasquez shouted. "You son of a bitch!"

"Oh, come on, now, no one likes a lady with a filthy mouth," Michael said. He pulled a key from his pocket and unlocked the shackles around Richie's wrists.

"Let this be a lesson to all of ya. We'll treat ya nice if you stay in line. Try and pull some nonsense like this boy did, and you see what happens. Okay? Everyone get it? Good. Joseph, come on and help me get his body out of here."

Alex watched in fury as the two men pulled Richie's corpse out of the room. His jaw and fists clenched. He barely heard the hateful mutterings of his companions, or the fearful sobbing of some of the civilians in the room. Richie had been a good kid, polite and respectful, and by all accounts a decent soldier. He had barely been out of high school, for Christ's sake. And this bastard just straight up murdered him.

Alex's eyes narrowed. One thought filled his head as he watched Michael close the door of the garage.

I'm going to kill him.

* * *

Alex didn't know how long it was before the door opened again. This time it was Ann who entered, carrying a bucket.

"Got some meat for ya," she said, motioning to the bucket in her hand. "I ain't got time to portion it out, so you'll have to divvy it up for yourselves. Try and be fair, now."

Alex looked around and saw the other prisoners were mostly asleep. All his companions were awake, but kept still, eyeing the woman who'd drugged them.

153

"Ann," Alex said. "You're making a terrible mistake."

She snorted. "That a fact?"

"I know you think you're doing what you have to in order to protect your son. But this . . . this isn't the answer."

"Really. And you got all the answers, I suppose."

Alex laughed, but there was no humor in it. "Hardly. I don't think any of us do. But I can tell you one thing I know for sure. If the human race is going to survive through this, we all have to stick together. Support each other. Help each other. When we all start turning on our fellow human beings and crying 'every man for himself,' then the Seraphim have as good as won."

"And there's more than just the Seraphim," Vasquez said. "There's a whole other race of aliens, the Malakhim, that came here wanting to steal our water. So even if you did get the Seraphim to agree to your deal and leave you alone, you'll still be fucked, because you won't have any water to stay alive with."

Ann looked from Alex to Vasquez and back again. "Yeah, right," she said.

"It's true," Matthews said. "Unless each and every one of us work together, there's no future for the human race."

"And you'd be willing to work with us, would you?" Ann said, smirking. "Even after my husband went and shot your friend."

Alex clenched his jaw, swallowing his anger. "Even then," he said. It was a lie, of course. He fully planned on getting his revenge on Michael. But he would say anything to save his people.

"Let me tell you something," Ann said, looking at all of them. "There was a time, way back when, when I'd have believed y'all. I used to think the military that protected us was the finest institution on God's green earth. Now, me and Michael, we never made that much money, but whenever we had a little to give, you can bet your ass we gave to the military charities. Our boys fighting for us deserved at least that much."

"So what changed your mind?" Hartinger asked.

"What the hell do you think?" she said. "Aliens! Now I know sure as hell you can't look me in the eye and tell me that y'all didn't know these things existed before they attacked us. Huh? Am I right?"

Hartinger looked at the floor. "You're right. Some of us knew, ma'am. But most of the military didn't—"

Ann stomped the floor in anger. "Of *course* ya knew! You think we don't know that? Everyone knows the damn government does nothing but lie to us. Always has, always will." She laughed. "Or I guess I should say 'always would have,' 'cause I don't think the government is in any position to lie these days, huh?"

"There is no government," Alex said. "Not any-more. And there won't be for a good long time, if ever again. We need to govern ourselves now."

Ann leaned closer to him. "That's exactly what we're doing."

She stood up and nudged the bucket closer to them, and then turned to leave.

"Ann," Alex said.

She turned and looked at him, her hands on her hips. "What?"

"Be better than this," he said. "Let us out of here. We'll help you. We'll get you to safety."

She shook her head. "Only safety now is the safety we make for ourselves. Sorry, y'all. You're food for the aliens now. Better start making your peace with that, because that ain't gonna change." She walked out and closed the door behind her.

All was silent for a moment, and then Vasquez said, "What a bitch."

"But useful," Hartinger said quietly.

Alex turned to him. "Useful how?"

"Didn't you guys see? She was wearing a key around her neck. She tried to keep it in her shirt, but it came out when she bent down to move the bucket. And I have a good idea of what that key opens." He raised his manacled wrists.

Matthews perked up. "I noticed Michael and the kids have tiny chains around their necks, too. No doubt they all have keys. If we can get one of them close enough . . ."

"Yeah. *If*," Alex said glumly.

"Keep your head up, marine," Hartinger said. "Everything is a puzzle. We just found the most important piece."

Alex tried to let that lift his spirits, but it was no good.

* * *

Alex's head rolled to the side and he awoke with a start. He didn't know how long he'd been sleeping. He didn't even know what time of day it was. Here in the dark of the garage, time had lost all meaning. Had they been there for a day? Two? Three?

He remembered learning about all kinds of torture techniques, and one that struck him as perhaps the most cruel was simply neglect. You took a prisoner and left him in a dark room with no space to move around and only the barest amount of food and water to survive. The mind plays all sorts of tricks when left to its own devices without external stimulation. It's one of the reasons, Alex knew, that solitary confinement was such an effective sanction in prisons. Solitude leads to dread.

Here, at least, he had companions, but that provided little comfort. Just as he was beginning to surrender to despair, he heard motion beside him.

"Hey," came Vasquez's voice.

"Can't sleep?" Alex asked.

"Somehow these accommodations aren't quite up to my standards," she said.

"Well, you always were a high-maintenance kind of girl."

Vasquez laughed. "Totally."

Alex looked around the room. "This can't be it," he said. "We haven't come this far, lost so many of our people, only to end like this. Outsmarted by some fuckwads in the middle of nowhere. We're smarter than this. We're marines, for fuck's sake."

"Oorah," Vasquez said without enthusiasm.

They sat there for a moment in silence, and then Alex said, "I can't believe they killed Richie."

"Fuck," Vasquez spat. "I know. That poor kid."

"I'm going to kill Michael," Alex said.

In his peripheral vision, he saw Vasquez turn to him in surprise. "Shephard," she said. "That kind of talk isn't like you."

"Maybe it is now," Alex said. "The whole world's turned upside down. Hell's come to earth. Nothing is what it used to be."

"That doesn't mean you're a cold-blooded killer."

Alex grimaced. "He has to be stopped."

"Agreed," Vasquez said. "And we'll stop him. Somehow. We'll get out of this. But we'll do it the right way. The way of the law, like we swore to uphold. If not, we're no better than the Seraphim and you know it."

Alex bent his head down. His rage against everything—Michael, the situation they were in, the Seraphim, the Malakhim—burned hot within his chest. He wanted to scream. He knew deep down Vasquez was right, but it brought him no solace.

"Wait," Vasquez said. "Do you hear that?"

"What?" Alex asked. He didn't hear anything.

Vasquez put a finger to her lips and hissed, "It sounds kind of like thunder."

Alex strained to hear. At first he still heard nothing, but then he caught it. A rumbling in the distance.

"It's not thunder, though, is it?" Vasquez said.

"No . . ." Alex said. Others began stirring. Again there was a rumble in the distance, followed by the vaguest vibration underneath them. For a split second, Alex thought it might be an earthquake, and then he realized how foolish that was. All the signs that pointed to an earthquake belonged in the old world. This world was new. This world had alien ships. And Alex suddenly knew what the rumbling in the distance was.

But it was Hartinger who whispered the words. "They're coming."

Alex felt his pulse quicken. He had no doubt it was true. The muffled sounds in the distance were eerily familiar to him, and they brought him right back to the night that Camp Lejeune fell to the Seraphim forces. The monsters were real, and they were coming back.

The prisoners who had been there before Alex's group began whimpering and pulling at their chains even as Alex heard Joseph shrieking for his parents.

"Come look! Come look!" his voice resounded through the door.

"I'll be damned." It was Michael speaking now. "Y'all remember the plan now."

Alex heard Ann begin to speak, but whatever she said was cut off by a deafening hum, followed a split second later by a bright yellow ray exploding through the garage ceiling. Splintered wood and rubble flew everywhere, and the bright morning sun suddenly flooded the putrid room with light. Alex squinted in the glare. He looked up through the hole in the roof just in time to see a giant Seraphim airship float above them.

"Holy fucking shit," he said.

It had been a while since he'd seen an actual spaceship. Most of their encounters with the Seraphim were just with their individual attackers. Seeing the behemoth that was their vehicle gliding through the air like a monster out of an ancient myth shook him to his core.

Around him was chaos. Dust and debris rose up in a cloud, and many of the prisoners were screaming. He heard Ann scream Michael's name, then more indecipherable shouting on the other side of the door.

"We're sitting ducks here," Hartinger said. "We've got to get free."

"Why would they use a ship to attack the ground? It doesn't make any sense. There's nothing here that causes a threat to them."

"Doesn't really matter right now, does it?" Alex said.

They all strained against their chains, but it was no good. They were stuck to the wall and weren't going anywhere. And with the gaping hole now open in the ceiling, they were fully exposed to the Seraphim.

There was another large hum, followed by the sound of an explosion. Alex knew the ship must have unleashed another ray. A bloodcurdling scream came from outside, followed by "No! No! No!"

"Jesus Christ, what's going on out there?" Rachel, the Johnsons' farmhand, asked.

"Don't rightly know, ma'am," Hartinger said. "I'm a little worried we're about to find out, though."

Suddenly all grew quiet. But the silence only lasted for about half a minute. Then more hums and throbbing tones filled the air, followed by the sounds of explosions. Alex heard footsteps coming towards the door, and then it burst open, revealing Joseph standing in the frame. His eyes were wild. He stared at all of them, his chest heaving with each raspy breath.

"What's going on?" Rachel screamed.

"The fucking aliens killed my parents!" he shouted, his voice high and hysterical. "They're dead! They're both dead!" With shaking hands, Joseph pulled a pistol out of the back of his pants and aimed it at all of them.

"Whoa, now!" Alex said. "Put that away, kid. We can help you get out of here, but you have to set us free!"

"Don't you fucking lie to me, asshole!" Joseph screamed.

"I'm not!" Alex said. "We can help you!"

But from the sight of the boy's face, Alex knew there was no getting through to him. He was in full panic mode, having just witnessed the death of the only two people who represented any idea of safety to him. His skin was pale and he kept clenching and unclenching his jaw, as he paced around like a wild animal trapped in a cage.

This could get even worse real fast, Alex thought. If Joseph felt like there was no safety left to him, it was very probable that he was likely to shoot all of the prisoners and then take himself out as well. It was a textbook hostage situation gone wrong.

"All right, listen to me now, Joseph," Alex said, making sure to use the boy's name. That was basic crisis psychology—people often responded to the sound of their own names. "I know this is scary as all hell . . ."

"You're fucking right it is!" Joseph screeched. He marched up to Alex and pressed the barrel of his gun against Alex's forehead. Alex's companions shouted in protest.

"You know what I think?" Joseph said. "I think since you all seem to know so much about the aliens, you must be working with them! You all tricked us!"

Before Alex could respond, he saw a flurry of motion in his peripheral vision: Vasquez lunged forward as far as she could given her restraints and aimed a powerful kick at Joseph's hand. The gun went flying out of his hand and landed harmlessly on the other side of the room, skidding away in a spiral. Alex, reacting with all of his training, lashed out with a foot and swept Joseph's legs out from under him, striking him hard on the ankle and pushing as hard as he could. The boy's leg flew high and he toppled to the ground on his butt with his back to Hartinger. The CIA agent, without skipping a beat, wrapped his legs in a triangle choke hold around Joseph's neck, trapping his throat with the calf of one leg and hooking the foot underneath the other knee. The boy kicked and thrashed and struggled against Hartinger's ironlike vise grip, but it was no use. There was no way he was breaking free.

"Let me go!" Joseph rasped.

"Give us the key!" Alex shouted.

"What key?"

"Don't play stupid, kid. Seriously, now is not the fucking time. Give me the key you have around your neck."

"I don't know what you're talking about, you son of a bitch!"

Alex squinted at him. "Hartinger," he said, glancing at the man with a significant look. "Break his neck."

It was a bluff. Even in the direst of circumstances, he knew Hartinger wouldn't do it. Hartinger nodded, indicating he was in on the plan, and moved his hips, squeezing just the slightest bit.

It was enough. The ruse worked.

"No! Stop!" Joseph pleaded. "All right! All right! I'll let you out. Just don't kill me!"

"Good choice, kid," Hartinger said.

He relaxed his legs just a bit, and Joseph reached into his shirt and pulled out the chain underneath, complete with dangling key. He yanked at the chain and the clasp came undone.

"Here's the key," he said.

"Toss it on the ground over here," Alex commanded. Joseph obeyed, and lobbed the key in his direction. It slid right up to Alex's boot. He grabbed it with his heel and pulled it towards his hands. Then he seized the key and unlocked the manacles around his wrists.

Finally free, he unlocked Matthews and Vasquez, and handed the key to them as he turned on Joseph. More explosions resounded outside, and Alex cringed. It sounded more and more like a battle. He didn't know what was going on, but he knew they had to get out as soon as possible.

"You can let him go, Hartinger," he said, and Hartinger released his chokehold. Alex stared the boy down. "I know this wasn't your fault. You were going by what your folks told you to do."

"My folks are dead because of you, asshole!" Joseph screamed, tears of anger springing from his eyes.

"You know that's not true, kid," Alex said. "I'm not going to lie. The world's gone to shit, and that didn't have anything to do with us or your parents. But the aliens are here now, and we've got to deal with that. And look, kid, we're going to get out of here. Come with us. We can help you. We can give you protection in our bunker."

As Vasquez and Matthews freed the last of the prisoners, Joseph looked up at Alex with desperate eyes. It was clear he was still in shock at the death of his parents. He had nobody now, and Alex offered him safety in a world full of lethal danger.

"Even after all this?" he croaked.

"Even after all this," Alex said. "We'll keep you safe."

"Like hell you will," a voice came from the other side of the room. They all turned to see Rachel holding the gun that Vasquez had kicked out of Joseph's hands. She pointed it right at Joseph.

"Oh, for fuck's sake!" Alex said. "We don't have time for this! Do you hear what's happening outside?"

As if on cue, a thunderous explosion roared close to them, and everyone in the room flinched. The sound couldn't have been more than two hundred yards away.

"This dipshit helped his parents lock us all up!" Rachel screamed, frantic. "He doesn't deserve to be saved! Leave him here!"

"Right now we need to focus on keeping every human safe, Rachel," Matthews said, keeping his voice calm and even. "We can sort everything else out later, back at the base. But we need to get out of here, and that's going to take all of us working together. Put the gun down."

Rachel looked around with wild eyes. Alex knew she was dealing with the immediate aftermath of captivity, and had no military training to help her deal with the psychological trauma. She was losing it, and that plus a gun was a dangerous combination.

Vasquez, it seemed, had drawn the same conclusion. She crept up silently behind Rachel, then sprang to her side, grabbed her wrist, and brought it high in the air. She then pivoted and brought down her other elbow, pinning Rachel's arm to her side. All it took was a little pressure, and she dislocated the farmhand's shoulder, causing her to immediately drop the gun. Rachel howled in pain and clutched her shoulder.

"Sorry about that," Vasquez said, picking up the gun and tucking it into the back of her pants. "But like Shephard said, we don't have time for this."

"All right, everyone, listen up!" Alex shouted. "We've got one mission right now, and that's to get out of this alive. That means we all work together, no matter what our grievances right now. Understood?"

Rachel, cradling her shoulder, solemnly nodded, as did Joseph and the other prisoners. With Alex in the lead, they approached the door that led out of the garage. Alex found the button on the wall that lifted the door, and pressed it. Slowly, the door creaked up, exposing the outside world.

Alex's breath caught in his throat.

A Seraphim ship hovered two hundred feet above the ground, smoke emanating from a large hole in its side, the charred outline showing signs of some kind of weapon fire. Bright blasts came from the ship intermittently, some towards the ground, some in the air around it. It was then that Alex saw other, smaller ships buzzing around the Seraphim ship like flies, unloading their own fire at the larger craft.

There was a deafening mechanical groan, and the Seraphim ship started losing altitude.

"Shit, it's going down!" Hartinger said.

"What the fuck is going on?" Alex whispered, looking at the scene in front of him. It was so surreal, even after all he'd witnessed. He felt like he was watching a movie, like the events in front of him were removed from reality.

But deep down he knew this was real. And they were all in danger. Perhaps more danger than he'd ever been in before.

"It's the Malakhim," Matthews said. "Those smaller ships—they're the Malakhim's attack vessels they use when they engage in planet-based dogfights. They favor maximum maneuverability over brute force."

"Oh, great!" Vasquez said. "So how the hell do we get past them?"

"We run," Alex said.

"Shephard, it's fucking War of the Worlds out there," Vasquez said.

"Yeah. I know. But staying here isn't an option." He turned and looked at everyone behind him and was met with looks of dread. But he knew it was the only way.

"Where are we running to exactly?" Vasquez asked.

Alex bit his lip and tried to remember the layout of the land. There was the main house that was attached to the garage, and the barn about three hundred yards away. Michael had parked the van on the other side of the barn. It occurred to Alex that if they were going to get away, that's where they had to do it.

"We take their vehicle," he said. "The van. It's big enough to carry all of us."

"Good plan," Hartinger said.

Alex nodded curtly. "Ready?"

On the nods of his companions, Alex turned back to the scene before him.

"Let's go!" he called.

He took off at a sprint, and was vaguely aware of everyone running behind him. Almost immediately, the earth next to him was hit by a stray beam and exploded in a hectic cloud of dirt, grass, and rocks. Alex ducked and covered his face, but wasn't able to prevent small bits of matter getting into his eye. He squinted in pain, but continued his sprint.

A scream behind him made him turn around, and he saw that one of the male prisoners whose name he'd never learned had taken a direct hit from one of the Seraphim's rays. The blast had bifurcated his torso before he'd had a chance to make a noise. The scream had come from one of the other prisoners.

Alex grimaced, but knew this wasn't the time to mourn the man. "Keep going!" he urged.

"But . . . but Philip . . ." one of the prisoners protested.

"There's nothing we can do for him now!" Alex shouted. "Come on! We have to keep moving!"

Reluctantly, the prisoners followed his orders. As Alex turned back around, he was suddenly rendered motionless by the awful sight before him. Frozen in place, he watched as the Seraphim airship crashed into the barn, seemingly in slow motion, as the Malakhim attack ships swarmed around it. Laser beams and dust flew through the air as the gargantuan vessel dug into the earth, and the creak of shattered wood was deafening.

"The barn . . ." Alex whispered.

Exactly where the Johnson's van was parked. That was their way out, and now it was gone.

"Shit!" Vasquez said. "Now what?"

"We find another vehicle," Alex said, not giving himself time to despair. They had one objective—escape—and he was not going to fail them. "Keep moving, everyone! Follow me!"

He veered off to the right to go around the Seraphim's ship, and as they sprinted on, Alex saw something that made his heart stop. A familiar rectangle of light appeared on the side of the ship, and then the metal inside the shape shimmered and seemed to evaporate, opening a door into the interior. Out of this door flew dozens of Seraphim, their hands already glowing with their percussive energy, just waiting to be unleashed in blasts.

"Oh, fuck . . ." Alex muttered.

Hartinger screamed "Everybody take cover!" as the Seraphim emerged. The aliens didn't seem to notice the small band of humans on the ground, as their attention was on the attacking Malakhim ships. They began blasting away at the vessels, which returned fire on the Seraphim as they soared through the air like eagles. Alex pulled one of the other prisoners down behind a hay bale just as a stray blast from one of the Malakhim ships almost took his head off. Matthews scurried over to where Alex was hunched down.

"We've got to get out of here!" Alex shouted to be heard over the exchange of fire. "We're sitting ducks!"

Alex looked over and tried to find his companions through the smoke and laser fire. Everyone had ducked behind some form of shelter, mostly hay bales and a few scattered pieces of farm equipment. He locked eyes with Vasquez and Hartinger, and the wordless communication was clear: get away as fast as possible.

Alex looked up at the hideous sight of the Seraphim flying on the power of their jetpacks and engaging with the Malakhim ships. There was a huge volley of fire. The moment it ended, he screamed, "Now!" He leaped up and raced away, choosing a direction at random, and everyone followed. But once again they were cut off. They hadn't made it even a hundred feet before a Seraphim landed in their path. As it plummeted to the ground, Alex jumped back, prepared for an assault. But he immediately realized this was unnecessary. The Seraphim landed on its side and rolled limply a few times before coming to a stop, and Alex saw that half of its face was blown off.

Unfortunately, the dead one was followed by a Seraphim who was very much alive. It landed on its feet with a loud thud and stared at Alex with its terrifying, emotionless face.

Alex gaped as two things occurred to him at once—the Seraphim in front of him was charging up the laser in its hand, and another alien was flying toward them. As the first Seraphim took aim at him, Alex sprang forward, grasped its wrist, and pointed it at the approaching flier. Taken by surprise, the first Seraphim didn't react quickly enough, and before it could stop itself the laser blasted its companion, hitting the creature straight in the chest. As the flier tumbled onto the ground face down, clearly dead, the Seraphim roared and struck Alex with the back of its hand. Alex was thrown ten feet away and crashed into Hartinger, who'd been rushing to help.

He'd forgotten how hard the Seraphim could hit. Through his haze, he watched numbly as Vasquez and Matthews leaped onto the Seraphim's back. Matthews, Alex saw, had held onto the chain that had bound him to the pipe inside, and he wrapped this around the Seraphim's throat and pulled hard. Vasquez, meanwhile, banged viciously on the creature's head with a small object. Alex realized it was a wrench, and figured she must have picked it up somewhere in the field, most likely near one of the pieces of farm equipment. The Seraphim continued stalking toward him with the two humans on its back. But finally it succumbed to their blows, staggered, and fell to its knees. Its hand began to glow, and Alex knew he had only seconds to react.

"Hold him down!" Alex shouted. Matthews pulled back with all the strength he had, and the Seraphim collapsed on top of him, its back on his front, Matthews still clinging to the chain wrapped around its neck.

Alex shouted as he lunged for the Seraphim, "Vasquez, out of the way!" Vasquez leaped away, and just in time, Alex grabbed the Seraphim's hand, turned it towards itself, and watched with a sickening satisfaction as the thing blasted its own face off.

Hartinger appeared next to him and helped him shove the thing off of Matthews. "Good team work," he said. "Now we have to figure out a way to get as far from these fuckers as possible and fast. On foot's not gonna do it."

Rachel had run up to them following the death of the Seraphim. "There's another farm on the other side of those trees," Rachel said, and pointed to a wall of trees in the distance, just past the smoldering wreck of the Seraphim airship. "They might have left a vehicle or two."

"That's our only shot, then," Alex said. "I'm not looking to die here today. Let's go!"

With renewed energy, the group sprinted towards the trees Rachel had pointed to, trying to tune out the battle being fought just above them. Twice, Alex heard the deadly sizzle of an alien laser nearby, followed by shrieks and the sounds of bodies hitting the ground. He knew without looking they had lost two people, and selfishly prayed that neither of them were Vasquez, Hartinger, or Matthews. The time they could slow their escape to check on their dead was long past. He would have to wait until they reached the safety of the trees to be sure.

A beam landed right in front of him, exploding the earth beneath it, and Alex jumped straight through the cloud of dirt that erupted in its wake. He felt a fire burning in his lungs and ran all the faster. He was running for his life now. He was running to survive, not only for himself but for Kate, and their unborn child. He was running for his family. So he put his head down and sprinted faster than ever before in his life.

The trees were closer now. Fifty feet away. Thirty. Ten. And then he was inside. Even though tree branches were no match for an alien blast, he thanked fate for even that tiny bit of shelter. It was a narrow strip of woods, and when he emerged on the other side, he saw a truly wonderful sight. There, farther down the field from where he stood, was a van parked near a barn. The van wasn't quite as large as the one that had belonged to the Johnsons, but with a grimace, Alex realized they were three less in number now than when they'd left the scene of their captivity. The van would be enough.

Alex turned and saw the others come through the trees. He breathed a sigh of relief when he saw Vasquez, Matthews, and Hartinger. Rachel came after them, followed by a few of the men. It saddened Alex that he couldn't remember the faces of the men who'd just died, and he'd never even learned their names.

"Come on, head to the van!" he shouted, and everyone complied. He looked up over the hedge of trees and saw that the air battle was as ferocious as ever. But at least they were finally getting away. He ran with the others across the field to the van, and he got there just as Hartinger opened the door and searched for a key.

"Nothing," he said. "I think I'm going to have to hot wire it. This'll take a few minutes."

"Okay, you get on that," Alex said. "Everyone inside the van! Now! I'm going to do a search in the barn to see if I can find a key and save us some time."

"Roger that," Hartinger said, already scouring the van for a makeshift tool to use.

Alex sprinted towards the barn. He raced through the half-open door and looked around. Then there was a quick *whoosh* behind him, followed by a splitting pain on the back of his head. He staggered to the ground and grasped the back of his skull. Immediately he felt blood. Confused, he rolled over and looked up. He saw Michael standing over him, bloody and pale, holding a length of metal pipe.

"You knew this would happen, you son of a bitch," he slurred, limping towards Alex. "'Cause of you, my wife is dead. I watched her die from one of them laser blasts."

"Michael," Alex said, "we tried to warn you . . ."

"Tried to save your own skin, you mean," Michael said, swinging the pipe around, building momentum. "Now I'm gonna make sure you end up just like my wife."

Alex took in the sight of him. He looked half-dead, with a staggering gait, and blood and bruises covering his body. But there was fire in his eyes as he swung the pipe, and Alex knew with no uncertainty that Michael would do everything he could to kill him. He bared his teeth and swung the pipe high, bringing it down hard. Alex rolled out of the way just in time and shot a kick out at Michael's shin. The man cried out in pain from the blow and dropped to one knee, but quickly swung the pipe at Alex again in a fast arc. The metal whizzed by Alex's face, missing him by an inch.

Michael's third swing hit home.

Alex felt the impact of the pipe against his ear, and for a few seconds there was no pain. Then it all came at once, blinding and crushing. He could hear nothing but a dull throbbing in his skull, and he felt the warm drip of blood on his neck. He was on his side, but fell onto his back, unable to stand. Michael raised the pipe once again, and Alex knew he meant this to be a killing blow. Summoning every last reserve of strength he had, he lifted both legs and caught Michael's neck between his ankles. He rolled over as fast as he could, wrenching the other man down onto the floor of the barn. Alex was able to pull himself up on top of him, and then he rained down punches on the other man's face and head until he stopped moving. Alex pulled himself onto his knees, then staggered to his feet and picked up the pipe. He looked down at Michael, conscious but hurt, and in his mind's eye he saw the man shoot Richie once again in cold blood.

Alex's fingers curled and tightened around the pipe. *It would be so easy,* he thought. *Just bring the pipe down on his head and end it.*

He was going to do it to you.

He killed Richie.

Do it.

But as he stood there, the pipe ready in his hands, Alex realized he couldn't do it.

He tried. He pictured himself lifting the pipe and smashing it down on Michael's skull. He knew exactly the speed, force, and angle needed to end his life immediately, with no suffering. But he couldn't bring his arm to obey his commands.

Not sure of what to do, Alex turned and walked unevenly out of the barn. Once outside, he saw that the battle between the Seraphim and Malakhim forces was spilling over onto their side of the trees, and his companions were waving to him frantically from the van, which hummed with life. Hartinger had been successful in hot-wiring it.

"Shephard, let's go!" Matthews yelled from the van.

Alex moved as fast as he could, watching in fear as lasers from the Malakhim ships came ever closer. When he was halfway between the barn and the van, he heard Joseph yell out, "Pa!"

Alex turned around and saw Michael was following him, looking even more haggard than before.

"I'm'a kill you . . ." he slurred, coming closer to Alex.

Alex instantly regretted the mercy he'd shown him, and raised his pipe defensively . . . just

as a stray blast from one of the ships struck Michael directly in the torso. The man crumpled and fell, and Alex knew that this time he'd be staying down.

"*Pa, no!*" Joseph shrieked. Alex rushed to the van and hopped inside as the others restrained a now-hysterical Joseph. As soon as Alex was in, Hartinger hit the gas, and they tore away at a furious speed. Everyone inside the van besides Hartinger turned and watched the battle still playing out behind them. Alex whispered a prayer of thanks as the Seraphim fliers and Malakhim ships diminished with every foot they put between their escape vehicle and the battle. Before long, they could no longer see the battle at all.

Alex turned back around and sighed. Near him, Joseph continued his wailing, to the irritation of the other prisoners.

"Can someone shut him the fuck up, please?" Rachel said bitterly.

"My pa's dead!" Joseph screamed.

"Your pa was a psychopath," Rachel retorted. "Your ma, too, and so are you, most likely." She turned to Alex. "I don't know what the hell you were thinking, bringing him with us."

Alex looked at her, and then saw she was still cradling her shoulder where Vasquez had injured her. "Your shoulder's dislocated," Alex said, ignoring her words. "I can pop it back in place for you. It'll hurt like hell, but you'll be glad I did it."

"Christ," Rachel said. But she nodded stoically. As Joseph moaned in misery in the back of the van, Alex shuffled over next to her on the seat and instructed her to turn her back to him. "Anyone have anything she can bite down on?"

"Why do I need to bite down on something?" Rachel asked.

"You'll know soon enough."

One of the other prisoners produced a leather wallet out of his pocket and offered it to Alex. "How's this?" he asked.

Alex took it. "It'll have to do," he said, and gave the wallet to Rachel, who took it with a look of dread. "It's best to just get it over with quickly. Turn around and press your front against the seat back. And bite down on the wallet."

Rachel did as he instructed, and then Alex got behind her and placed his hands on her back. "Ready? One, two—" And then he pushed, and Rachel screamed through her clamped teeth.

"I hope it hurts, bitch," Joseph said, rocking himself back and forth and staring at her with daggers in his eyes.

The wallet fell out of her mouth, and tears poured from her eyes. "Fuck you!" she yelled at him.

"That's enough!" Matthews said. "Seriously, people. I know there's no love lost between you, and you're not going to patch things up and be friends any time soon, but we have to start working together now. All of us."

"He *imprisoned* us!" Rachel protested.

"He was following his parents' orders," Matthews pointed out. "They're the ones that imprisoned you."

"Oh, please, he could have gotten us out if he wanted to. He could have freed us in the middle of the night when those two evil fuckers were asleep."

"You're right," Alex said. He looked at Joseph. "She's right. You did some very bad things, kid, and you're going to have to answer for them. But later." He addressed them all. "Right now, we all have one objective, and that is the survival of the human race. That takes priority over everything. Get it?"

"But—"

"Did you not see that battle back there?" Alex said, his voice rising. "You saw what we're up against. What they're capable of. They're real life monsters from fucking outer space, and they're here to eradicate the human race. So suck it up, because I wouldn't care if Jeffrey fucking Dahmer is part of the team right now. We are sticking together and making sure our species survives this. Got it?"

Rachel grumbled a response and nodded. Joseph just looked out the window. The small sense of relief about being away from the battle was replaced with the grim atmosphere of worry for what lay ahead. Alex looked around at the taut faces and shook his head.

It was one thing to survive the aliens. But survival wasn't enough. Humanity needed to live again. And the first step was coming together.

They drove mostly in silence all the way back to Fort Hood, all of them grateful that they saw no other aliens the entire way. Alex's thoughts drifted to his time in the Johnsons' captivity, and how he had burned with hatred whenever he'd seen Michael following Richie's death. He had resolved to kill him, but when the opportunity came, he'd spared his life. He wondered why. Despite Kate's suggestion that God oversaw the Seraphim's plan, Alex had trouble actually continuing his belief in Heaven or Hell, or an all-powerful God who would protect his good children and punish those who did wrong. There was no reason for him to think that killing was a sin anymore, if indeed it was for the greater good—and killing Michael would definitely have been for the greater good.

Why, then? Why did he show him mercy?

Ultimately, Alex concluded that it must have been the sheer fact that Michael was, if nothing else, human. He wasn't an alien. He didn't come from space. He was of this planet.

And creatures like that were in short supply these days.

"Are y'all gonna arrest me?" Joseph said suddenly.

"What?" Alex said.

"You know," Joseph continued, "are y'all gonna put me in jail? For what I done to these people? I mean, y'all are in charge now, right? I can't go to jail. I'd never survive there. My ma and pa told me that all the time growin' up, whenever I got caught stealin' or whatever."

"Jail's not really, well, a *thing* anymore, kid," Alex said. "We have detainment facilities in Fort Hood, but the kind of jail you're talking about just no longer exists."

"Well, then, are y'all gonna put me in one of them? The detainment things?"

Alex sighed. "I don't know. We have what we call a command hierarchy, so my superiors will figure out what to do with you. But most likely they'll put you to work. Everyone's got to work together at the Fort, and we need every man we can get."

"You'd throw him in the detainment facility if you had any sense to you," Rachel said, and the other prisoners murmured their agreement.

"Yes, you've made your opinion quite clear, little lady," Hartinger said from the driver's seat. "There's no profit in keeping on pushing the point."

Alex was relieved when, at long last, he saw the silhouette of Fort Hood in the distance. They'd made it.

* * *

Alex opened his arms wide as Kate rushed into them.

"Oh, my God! Where were you? What happened?" she asked as tears stained her cheeks.

"A whole hell of a lot, babe," Alex said with a tired sigh. "But I can tell you this much. The apocalypse fucking sucks." On her questioning glance, he added, "I'll fill you in back in our room. We just have to talk to Conners."

"But—"

"I know. I don't want to do it either, but there's some things he needs to know. Go on, go back to the room. I'll join you there as soon as I'm done."

Kate wasn't happy about it, but she agreed. After an hour-long debrief with Conners, the Sergeant Major concluded that they'd hold Joseph in the detainment facility until he could prove he was trustworthy. The other prisoners would be patched up in the infirmary and then given a job once they'd healed. In the world before the Seraphim invasion, they would have been treated for psychological trauma, PTSD, and a whole host of other issues. But unfortunately, that wasn't the world they were living in anymore.

When Alex finally got to their quarters, he entered and sat on the bed, exhausted. He filled Kate in on everything that had happened since they'd left Fort Hood in search of the origin of the distress call. Kate gasped when he spoke of Richie's murder.

"But I don't understand," Kate said. "They rescued you from the Seraphim only to lock you up so they could *give* you to the Seraphim? That doesn't make much sense."

"We never saw the aliens from the first attack," Alex explained. "The Johnsons must have rigged a bomb on the road to make us think we were under attack, when really it was them all along."

"Jesus," Kate said, shaking her head. "I know it's naive to think that all human beings are good and all aliens are bad, but . . ."

"But you'd started to feel that way."

"Yeah. I did."

"Well, obviously we did, too," Alex said. "We walked right into their trap. You'd think with all the years of military training between us in that jeep, someone would have thought it suspicious that we never saw the aliens that were supposed to have been attacking us. Hell, even Hartinger and Matthews fell for it, and they're the elite of the elite."

Kate sat down next to him on the bed, her face solemn. "Just when you think you know who your enemies are . . ."

He took her hand. "As if this world couldn't get any more insane, right?"

She nodded, and he yawned. "Sorry," he said. "It's just forced captivity and almost getting beaten to death with a pipe kind of took a lot out of me."

He'd meant it as a joke, but she didn't laugh. In the military, everything was treated with gallows humor as a way of coping. But Kate was far too gentle a soul to find the humor in the situation. She kissed him softly on the cheek.

"Lay down, my love," she said, and Alex stripped off his clothes and got under the covers, grateful to be able to sleep in a bed instead of a filthy garage, even if the bed was just a standard-issue cot. Kate turned the light off and got into bed next to him. He wrapped one arm around her, placing the other hand on her stomach. Something inside her bumped against his palm, and in the dark Alex could sense Kate smiling.

"Did you feel that?" she asked.

"Yeah, I did," Alex said.

"We're a family," Kate said, and Alex drifted off to sleep.

For the next week, Alex spent what little free time he had with the other prisoners, making sure that they were acclimating to life in Fort Hood. He worried some of them would be too psychologically damaged by the horrors they had endured, and was prepared to let the staff know that some of them might have to be put on a suicide watch. But as it happened, every last one of them adjusted well. They were happy to be given tasks that made them feel useful in an environment with other human beings working to protect their species.

Even Rachel, who had been assigned to help in the infirmary, started to smile on a regular basis. When Alex came to visit Kate one day, he saw Rachel stacking boxes of supplies and approached her.

"How are you holding up?" he asked.

"I'm good," she said. "I . . . I want to apologize. For my behavior."

"Oh, no," Alex said, putting up his hands. "No apology necessary. There's not a person in this world who could blame you for feeling what you were feeling."

She sighed. "Are you a Christian, by any chance, Alex?"

"Well, that's a complicated question these days, but yeah, I suppose I am. I was brought up that way, at least."

"Me, too. And one of the things I remember the preachers always telling us is the power of forgiveness." She took a deep breath. "I've been struggling with it since we got out . . . but I know if I'm to live any kind of life, I have to forgive Joseph. So I'm making the decision to do just that."

Alex put a hand on her shoulder. "I'm proud of you, Rachel. I know that can't be easy."

Alex pondered his conversation with Rachel for the rest of the day. He met up with Vasquez to exercise in the Fort's gymnasium before dinner, and thinking of Rachel's words, he started to smile halfway through his set on the bench press.

Vasquez scoffed. "What's that grin for? Man, I don't even recognize your face when you're not scowling like a son of a bitch."

Alex laughed. "Rachel told me she's choosing to forgive Joseph."

"Huh," Vasquez said. "Think that means she'll also forgive me for dislocating her shoulder?"

"My guess is yeah."

"Well, that's a load off my mind."

Alex racked the barbell and sat up. "It's really something—the human spirit, isn't it?"

"Not getting all touchy-feely on me, are you?"

He laughed. "I just mean, with all the hell that's been unleashed on us, here we are. This fort is practically a city, and sure, there are still evil people like the Johnsons in the world. But not down here. Here, we're all working together. And if someone like Rachel can forgive someone like Joseph, well then . . . maybe we'll all end up being okay, after all."

Slowly, Vasquez's lips formed a smile. "You think?"

"Yeah," Alex said. "I'm kind of starting to."

At dinner that night, the first explosion came.

* * *

Alex was sitting with Kate at his side at a table with Vasquez, Hartinger, and Matthews. They were in the mess hall surrounded by the other inhabitants of the bunker and were deep in discussion about the Malakhim when they heard the sound and felt the vibrations pulse through the room.

Immediately, everyone sprang up from their seats. "Defensive positions!" someone cried out. "We've been discovered!"

Kate looked at Alex. Her face had gone deathly pale, and her hands instinctively covered her stomach. "They're here," she whispered.

Vasquez, Hartinger, and Matthews were already up and heading toward the center of operations.

"Vasquez!" Alex yelled out. When she whipped around, he shouted, "I'm getting Kate to safety. I'll meet you guys there."

Vasquez nodded and sprinted off.

"Come on, babe," Alex said. He took Kate's arm and led her down the hall in the direction of the infirmary.

"I was so stupid," Kate said as they hurried along.

"What are you talking about?"

"I actually started to believe we were safe here," she said. "But we're not safe. Nowhere's safe anymore, is it?"

Another explosion sent vibrations through the bunker.

"I don't think so," Alex said. "Come on. We've got to keep moving."

As they raced through the halls, Alex forced himself to fight off the feeling of despair. Without even knowing it, he had thought the same thing: this was a safe place for them to stay. Hidden, underground, reinforced. A stronghold for humanity.

But now it had been discovered.

They reached the infirmary and found the medical staff and some injured patients sitting there, their faces pale and terrified.

"Have we been infiltrated?" one of the doctors asked.

"No word on that yet, sir," Alex said, "but they're definitely outside."

A horrified murmur passed throughout the room. Alex turned to Kate. "I have to go. If we can secure a perimeter—"

"I know," Kate said. "Go."

Alex took off, sprinting back through the corridors to his quarters, where he grabbed the M16A4 assault rifle that had been issued to him after arriving at Fort Hood. He then ran to central command and found a crowd around Sergeant Conners, who was barking out orders, sending various factions to different areas of the bunker. At the back of the group he found Vasquez.

"Are they in?" he asked.

"Not yet," she responded. "But they're blowing their way through."

"The rest of you," Conners shouted, indicating Alex, Vasquez, and those near them, "get to the southern hangar and defend the entrances to the living quarters!"

Alex and Vasquez turned and rushed along with their fellow soldiers in the direction Conners had given them. Alex gripped his rifle and found it slippery—his hands were sweating.

Keep a cool head, he told himself. *Remember your training, Marine. These are just hostiles.*

And hostiles could be killed.

They moved together into the hangar, a cavernous space that housed at least a dozen small aircraft. Alex realized in wonder as they ran past them that one of these must be the alien ship that had been infamously discovered in Roswell, New Mexico, before being carted off by the feds. He'd never even given a second thought to the alien conspiracy theorists before, dismissing them as loony men who lived in their parents' basements. Now it turned out they'd been right all along.

Alex and the rest of the troops spread out in a single line, a solitary phalanx with their weapons raised. The hangar ended with a wide tunnel that led out to the field beyond Fort Hood, sectioned off by an enormous reinforced door. The tunnel was wide enough to accommodate small aircraft and tanks, but unfortunately that meant that if the Seraphim breached that entrance, they would be able to flood the room in seconds as opposed to minutes.

There was no superior officer with them, and so Alex took it upon himself to lead. "Hold tight, everyone!" he called out. "Hold this line. The Seraphim are vulnerable to head shots, so make 'em count."

"Oorah!" the men shouted in response.

Vasquez, standing next to Alex, turned her face to him and nodded. "Ooh fuckin' rah."

Alex nodded back and tightened his grip on his gun.

A loud banging sound came from the other side of the door to the tunnel, and everyone tensed up. They were outside.

"Hold the line!" Alex shouted again.

A loud sound came from behind the massive door. It was like the sizzle of steaks on a grill mixed with a serpentine hissing.

"They're cutting through," Vasquez shouted.

Alex knew they must be using whatever laser blasters they had attached to their hands. He had seen them cut through enough human beings with these tools to know the door wouldn't hold for very long.

"Here we go," he whispered.

With a metallic shriek, the door was ripped apart, and large pieces of jagged metal flew toward the soldiers. They retreated several yards to avoid being eviscerated, but one marine caught some shrapnel in his leg and went down with a harsh scream.

More Seraphim than Alex could count flew into the room, with even more coming behind them. "Fire!" Alex shouted.

The air was suddenly filled with the percussive staccato of bullets being fired mixed with the unworldly sizzle of the Seraphim's lasers. A stray laser hit one of the alien craft, causing it to explode. Smoke quickly filled the room. Alex lost sight of Vasquez in the chaos, her form becoming just one more silhouette against the murky cloud.

A Seraphim landed nearby with its back to him. Its hand began to glow as it took aim at a soldier. Alex shot it in the back of the head and watched with numb detachment as its head exploded, its brains and bits of skull flying out in a thousand different directions. The soldier that he saved didn't even know it, for he was locked in combat with three other Seraphim.

Alex whipped around, moving in a circle, keeping his weapon high. He picked off several hostiles with a few controlled bursts. So far, by some miracle, none of the Seraphim had targeted him, and he planned to use that bit of luck for as long as he could.

"Shephard!" he heard a high-pitched shriek from beside him. He turned and saw Vasquez barreling straight at him. Before he could stop her she smashed into him, knocking him down. He looked up just as she took a Seraphim's laser straight through her chest.

A laser meant for him.

Everything seemed to stand still for a moment, the hell that surrounded them frozen in time. In slow motion, Vasquez brought a hand up to the hole in her chest. She looked at Alex weakly, her eyebrows raised . . . and then she fell.

As her body hit the floor, her face slumped in Alex's direction, eyes open, her last expression one of abject terror.

"No!" Alex screamed.

The horrible injustice of it all crashed over Alex, a tsunami of fury and despair. They had come so far, lost so much, and through it all Vasquez had been a rock. She had made it with them, made it to what they thought was the safety of Fort Hood, only for her to die like this.

"*No!*" he screamed again, and let loose a torrent of fire on the alien that had struck the fatal blow. The creature was ripped apart by his bullets and was thrown down on its back, a bloody mess of meat and viscera.

Alex then unleashed his rage on every Seraphim he could see. They were everywhere. On the ground, in the air. All around him. But still he fired, destroying as many of their obscene lives as he could. Several of them attempted to subdue him with their blasts, but he dodged and wove through their fire. He saw a Seraphim land near him and squeezed the trigger but he was met with nothing but an empty metallic click. He was out of ammo. He charged the Seraphim, leapt into the air, and smashed the butt of his rifle right into its cold, unfeeling face, delighting when he heard the crack and crunch of bone and teeth. Just as that Seraphim slumped to the ground, Alex heard the sizzle of a laser behind him. There was a sharp pain behind his eyes, and then everything went black.

CHAPTER 10

At first, there was just darkness and a strange hum. Then a little light appeared at the center of his vision. Alex wasn't sure if his eyes were open or closed, for the light was blurred, like when you close your eyes and face the sun. He tried to speak, but no sound came out. He wasn't even sure if his mouth was moving.

He was conscious, and then he was not.

It happened again. And again. Darkness, then some light. Each time, the light was a little brighter, the field a little wider.

Finally, he saw shapes moving against the light. For a moment, he thought perhaps he was in heaven.

But no, he thought. If he was in heaven, he probably wouldn't be aware of his shoulder hurting like a motherfucker. "Wh . . . where . . ." he croaked.

A shape in the light stopped. Alex realized it looked vaguely human. *Please, God, let it be vaguely human, and not vaguely Seraphim.*

"Where . . ." he croaked again.

"He's awake," he heard someone say.

Vaguely human it is, then. Thank the Lord.

"Alex," he heard the voice say. "Alex, can you hear me?"

It was a woman's voice. Was it Kate?

"Alex? Come on now, Marine, let's see you open your eyes a bit more."

No. Not Kate. Someone else.

Alex couldn't feel his face, or at least he wasn't aware of feeling it, but he tried to open his eyes as the voice had instructed.

"There we go," the voice said.

His vision began to coalesce, infuriatingly slowly. A human shape was near his bed.

"Where . . ." he said, his voice just a whisper.

"You're safe."

Alex tried to make sense of this.

"I know you're probably disoriented," the voice said. "Right now we just need to get you back to the land of the living."

Alex tried to respond, but he was too confused.

"He's awake!" the voice called.

More shapes came into the light. They hovered above him. Alex realized he was lying down. "What . . . happened . . ." he rasped.

"You've been through quite an ordeal, son," a man's voice said.

Hartinger, Alex realized, though he couldn't see his face. He struggled to move, but felt gentle hands pressing him back down.

"You just concentrate on getting better. You were in a coma, and you've still got a nasty concussion. When you're up for it, we'll brief you. In the meantime, this here lady is Dr. Faith Kynlee. She'll be taking care of you."

"Where's . . . Kate . . ." he whispered, but the shapes had already left him.

* * *

Alex didn't know how long he had lain in the bed. It felt like years. And then, one day, he was able to sit up. The woman Hartinger identified as Dr. Kynlee came over to him. He saw that she was a middle-aged woman with dark brown hair tied in a messy bun. The room he was in was oddly rustic, with warm-toned wood paneling on the walls.

A cabin, he realized.

"How are you feeling, Alex?" she asked. She took out a penlight and shined it in his eyes.

Alex gripped her wrist, fast as a striking cobra. Kynlee gasped in shock.

"Where's Kate?" he asked.

"Who's Kate?" she responded. "Sorry, there's a few of you. I'm having trouble keeping track."

"My fiancée," Alex said. "Where is she? Who are you? What is this place?"

"I'll send for your friends," Kynlee said. "I'm sure they have all the info about your fiancée. But if we're going to move forward, I'm going to have to ask you to let go of me."

Alex slowly released his hold on her wrist.

"Thank you," she said.

"What the fuck happened to me?"

She sat on his bed and leaned toward him. "You were in a firefight. Do you remember?"

"A firefight . . ." Alex thought hard. It was like trying to remember a dream at first, something that disappears the more you try to clutch it. But then bits and pieces started to fill in. The Seraphim he killed. The sound of their lasers. And . . .

"Vasquez," he said. Tears filled his eyes suddenly, hot and painful.

"Vasquez?"

"Died. In the fight."

"He was a friend of yours?"

"She."

"I'm sorry."

Alex nodded. He bit his lip and swallowed hard. He wasn't about to cry in front of this strange woman. But he'd been through so much.

"Get Hartinger," he said. "I need to know what happened."

"Sure thing," Kynlee said.

Twenty minutes later, Hartinger walked into the room with Matthews in tow. "So you both made it," Alex said.

"We're tough guys," Matthews said. "Or so they tell us."

"Where are we?" Alex asked. "How did we get here? And where's Kate? I need to see her."

Hartinger and Matthews exchanged worried looks. Alex's face suddenly felt very hot.

"What?"

Hartinger sighed. "Shephard . . ."

"Hartinger. Where the fuck is Kate?"

"The Seraphim overwhelmed us," Hartinger said. "There were thirty of them for every one of our guys. Only nine of us made it out of Fort Hood. The rest were taken. I'm so sorry, Shephard. She's gone."

Alex looked at Hartinger for a few seconds, and then sprang up, knocking over a tray table covered with medical equipment. Seizing the man's arm, he shouted, "Don't you fucking lie to me, Hartinger!"

Kynlee, who'd been in a nearby room, came running in when she heard the crash. "Hey!" she yelled.

"It's all right, Doc," Hartinger said, holding his hand up to stop her.

"Calm down, Shephard," Matthews said, his tone soft. He put his hands around Alex's forearms, gently pulling him away from Hartinger.

"Don't tell me to calm down," Alex snarled. "Where was she taken? Where did they go? We have to get her. We have to get all of them."

"Listen, son," Hartinger said. "We're in a cabin a hundred odd miles away from Fort Hood, and we only made it here by the grace of God. There's a lot we have to tell you."

Just then, something appeared behind Hartinger, next to the doctor woman. Something enormous. Alex realized with a sick feeling what it was.

One of *them*.

He looked down at the ground, where the medical supplies had spilled. He swooped down and grabbed a scalpel, holding it up toward the alien.

"Shephard, *stand down!*" Hartinger shouted.

"Do not be afraid, friend Shephard," the creature said. Its voice was feminine. Alex realized it was Amitiel, the Malakhim whom they'd gone to see in Texarkana.

"You've got to be fucking kidding me," he said.

* * *

"I know it's a lot to take in," Matthews said.

He had taken Alex to a tiny bedroom, away from the others. Alex, who had almost hyperventilated upon seeing Amitiel, clenched his fists and forced himself to slow his breathing and calm down.

"A lot to take in?" he asked. "Are you fucking serious? We were attacked by aliens, my fiancée was taken, and now you're canoodling with the enemy? Give me one good goddamn reason I shouldn't kill everyone in this cabin right now."

"Well, you'd be pretty fucked if you did," Matthews said. "You still require medical attention, for one thing."

Alex frowned.

Matthews sighed and sat on the bed. "But the truth is Amitiel isn't our enemy."

"How can you say that?"

"She's not a Seraphim, Alex. She's not one of the invaders."

"She said they're here to take our fucking water! I'd say that's hostile."

"The Malakhim council ordered that, yeah. But Amitiel and her people are refusing. There's a rebellion going on among the Malakhim. That's what we saw when we were escaping from the Johnson's farm. The firefight between the Malakhim and the Seraphim, remember? Those ships were operating under Amitiel's orders. She's here to help us."

Alex snorted. "And you believe her? Why would she do that? Why would she care what the hell happens to mankind?"

"Because what's happening to us happened to them. They were invaded by the Seraphim, just like we're being invaded now."

"So we're just supposed to take her on her word that she disagrees with her higher-ups? I don't buy it."

Matthews threw his hands in the air. "Why? Because humans always agree with their governments?"

Alex wanted to respond, but realized he had no idea how to rebut that.

Matthews rested his hands on his knees. "Here's the thing, man. Not to sound like a sensitivity-training PSA, but the truth is these aliens are just as different from each other as humans. They're individuals. Some feel some way, some feel another. It's true for us, it's true for the Malakhim, and it's true for the Seraphim."

"The *Seraphim?*" Alex asked, his jaw dropping open. "Are you shitting me?"

"We've seen their military arm, yeah. The ones that follow orders. But that's all we've seen. It's like here on Earth, when there were German dissenters during Hitler's reign—people that spoke out and fought against the Nazis. This is the same thing."

Alex shook his head in disbelief. "I can't believe what I'm hearing."

"You can believe it or not, man. That's your choice. But it's the truth."

Alex hit himself on the sides of his head with both hands. "Why am I even here talking about this with you? I have to find Kate. I have to get her."

"Alex," Matthews said, infuriatingly gently. It was the first time he'd called him anything other than his last name. "You have to accept the fact that Kate's gone."

"Fuck you!" Alex shouted. "Fuck you, Matthews! You don't know that! You don't know what's happened to her."

"Actually, I do."

"*How?*"

Matthews looked away. "We're in touch with a cadre of American and Canadian military personnel. They've set themselves up in a bunker on the other side of the border. Apparently it's roughly the technological equivalent of what we had at Fort Hood. And they've been working—cooperating—with insurgents."

"Insurgents. You mean *them*."

"Malakhim and Seraphim who are human sympathizers, yeah."

Alex laughed humorlessly. "Fucking alien *spies*. Naturally."

"Their intel tells us that everyone taken at Fort Hood has been brought to one of their harvesting camps."

"What does that mean?"

Matthews was silent for a moment. "It's where they extract the blood."

A shiver passed through Alex just then, something he'd never experienced before. It was like all the warmth had just drained out of him. Images of Kate being manhandled, stuck with tubes, flashed through his mind.

"I'm going," he said. "I'm leaving right now."

"Shephard, you just came out of a coma."

"I don't give a shit!"

He clenched his fists again, and suddenly the world around him began to spin. The walls of the room almost seemed to bend. Dizzy, he asked, "What's happening to me?" as he tried to steady himself.

"Shephard?" Matthews said.

"I . . . I have to save her . . ." Alex said.

"Shephard, you're passing out. Just—"

Alex didn't hear Matthews finish his sentence.

CHAPTER 11

A lex blinked, and slowly the world began to come into focus again. His head was against a pillow, he could tell that much. His tongue felt gigantic in his mouth.

"Wha . . . happ'n . . ." he croaked.

"You fainted," a woman said. Alex realized it was Dr. Kynlee.

"I nee . . . nee . . . t'go . . ." he said, and tried to push himself up.

"God, what is with you?" Kynlee said, her voice flaring with irritation. "You're incapacitated. Got it? You can't go anywhere. You walked into another room and passed out, which should give you a good idea of your condition. That is, if you're not a complete moron, and to be honest the jury's still out on you. You're staying in that bed until I give you the all clear."

Alex opened his mouth groggily and moved his tongue around.

"You bit your tongue when you fainted," Kynlee said. "It happens a lot. The best way to let it heal is not to talk too much. So, really, we all win."

Alex scowled at her.

"And I'm serious about not getting out of that bed," Kynlee added. "You won't be good to anyone if you lose it after walking three feet. You need to heal. Okay, Marine? I mean it. That's an order."

She left, and Alex wished he had the energy to scream. But he was too weak.

He pushed his head back against the pillow, fighting the feelings of rage and despair. All he could think of was Kate and their unborn child. Was it possible they were still alive? Could he cling to that hope?

Days passed and they felt like years. Alex drifted in and out of consciousness, and often cursed Kynlee for being as strict as a nun with his pain meds. Matthews and Hartinger came to visit him, but they never had much to talk about with him, and he found their company didn't exactly lift his mood.

One day, he opened his eyes from sleep and jumped a bit. Amitiel, the Malakhim, was seated in a chair on the other side of his room. Even sitting down, she still far exceeded the height of a normal human being, and her white eyes terrified him.

"You are awake, friend Shephard," she said in her chilling monotone.

"What the fuck are you doing here?" he murmured.

"Fisher Matthews asked me to come speak to you."

"Why the fuck would he think I'd want to talk to *you?*"

"You do not trust me because I am Malakhim."

"That's right."

"I understand this. It is the nature of all life to be distrustful of what it does not know. This makes it easier to survive."

Alex looked at her. "Survive? That's a joke coming from you."

"I do not understand what you mean by this."

Despite the pain, Alex pushed himself up to a sitting position. "You and your monster family came here to take our water. Even if we are able to beat the Seraphim, you're making sure we won't survive. Aren't you?"

"That is the will of the Malakhim council. But it is not mine. I have chosen to defy them, as have some of my brethren. We are outcasts among our own people now, because we believe in what we are doing."

Alex lay back down and scoffed. "Why are you here? Why do you want to talk to me?"

Amitiel was silent for a moment. Then, "I would like to tell you a story."

Alex let out a mirthless chuckle. "A story. Really."

"It is a part of the history of the Seraphim. Therefore, it is also the history of the Malakhim . . . and the history of humans."

"You already told me. We're a fucking experiment."

"There is more. Fisher Matthews tells me that you are a devout follower of the Creator. The entity you call God."

Hearing her speak of God caused fury to well up deep within Alex's chest. It felt so wrong, so blasphemous to converse with her about such a thing. "I'm not going to talk about my faith with a goddamn alien," he spat.

"That is your choice, friend Shephard. But if you will not talk, perhaps you will listen. I believe you will be very interested in what I have to say."

Alex couldn't help but be intrigued but wasn't about to admit it. "Fine," he muttered.

"Fisher Matthews has explained to me that your collective understanding of man's creation is recorded in a book you call the Bible."

"Yeah," Alex said. "Well, I mean, not exactly."

Amitiel inclined her head. "Not exactly how?"

Alex rolled his eyes, disbelieving he was about to launch into a theological discussion with an alien. "It's not really our understanding, as least not literally. Our religious leaders teach that God created mankind in the form of Adam and Eve. The first humans. But I don't believe that's true."

"What do you believe?"

"I think the story of Adam and Eve is a metaphor. We know we evolved from lesser life forms, simpler organisms that eventually became reptiles, which became mammals, and so on. It was always my belief that humanity evolved as designed by God's hand. But now I know that's . . . it's fake. It's all fake, and the Seraphim put us here like the Earth is one giant fucking laboratory for them."

He looked away, and again Amitiel was quiet. When she spoke, her voice was barely a whisper. "Adam and Eve did exist, and there was a Garden of Eden."

Slowly, Alex looked over to her. "What?"

"That story is true. I cannot speak to all of the stories in your Bible, but I can attest to the veracity of that particular piece."

Alex shook his head. "No. That's impossible."

"Why do you say this?"

"Because we . . . we know we evolved! There's evidence. Mountains of evidence. We've seen evolution in our lifetimes. And besides, you said the Seraphim caused us to evolve!"

"They did."

"Then how was there a Garden of Eden? You're saying Adam and Eve were just plunked down, already evolved to the current state of mankind?"

Amitiel gently swayed her head. "Ah," she said. "I see that my phrasing was unclear. There was a Garden of Eden, but it was not here on earth. The location of the garden was on the Seraphim home world."

Alex gawked. "So . . . wait . . . so Adam and Eve . . ."

"They were the first Seraphim."

A wave of nausea overcame Alex. He didn't know if it was a result of his concussion or what Amitiel was saying. "I don't understand," he said. "If . . . if the Seraphim created the Malakhim and us, then who . . . ?"

"Your faith was not misplaced, friend Shephard. The Seraphim were created by he of many names, whom we most often call Elohim."

"Elohim . . ." Alex breathed.

"Yes," Amitiel said. "The one you call God."

The sound of the words on her alien lips made Alex shiver. She couldn't be telling him the truth.

Unless, impossible as it seemed, she was.

"I don't understand . . ." Alex muttered. "How . . . ?"

"Eons ago . . . an unfathomable expanse of time . . . He whom we call Elohim created the Seraphim. They were his children, and he loved them. He endowed them with great intelligence, the most useful aspect of which was their understanding of the other species on their planet. They saw evolution occurring, as guided by the hand of Elohim, though they themselves needed no such process.

"Over time, their intellect grew, which is when they began experimenting with the technology that has proven to be their bane. They became obsessed with eternal life, as I've spoken of to you before, which is how we all came to be in this situation now.

"Elohim, it is said, despaired that his once-beloved creations had become twisted, dark. They had lost their empathy for their fellow living creatures, as evidenced by the fact that they manipulated life on the Malakhim home world to evolve into us, a shadow of themselves, to be mined for our blood, and then repeated the process here on Earth.

"He was ashamed of the actions of the Seraphim, but could not bear to destroy them, Elohim withdrew from his first children. He is in a state of slumber now, a form of stasis called Ein Sof, somewhere beyond the scope of our understanding. He is both present on the Seraphim home world, and . . . not."

Alex shook his head, numb. "How do you know all this? It sounds like a fairy tale."

"It is recorded in the journals of the Seraphim's historians from all over their world. There is no interpretation, no disparities in the story from their many cultures. It is an undisputed fact."

Alex lay there for a moment, not knowing what to say. Amitiel stood. "I've given you much to think about, friend Shephard. I hope my words have brought you at least some comfort. Your faith is not misplaced."

With that, she rose and left his room.

2109

"I can't believe what I'm hearing," the younger man said.

"After all I've told you," the old man said, "it can't really be that surprising, can it?"

"Adam and Eve."

"Yes."

"The Garden of Eden."

"*Gan Eden*, the Seraphim called it. The word trickled down to us humans and was adopted by Jewish mystics. The kabbalah and all that. I'm sure you've heard of it."

The younger man just stared at him, open mouthed. "The kabbalah?"

The old man nodded and took a sip of whiskey.

"Yeah, I've heard of it."

"Well, there you have it. Turns out those mystics weren't so crazy after all."

The younger man looked from side to side, as though trying to shake his thoughts back together. "Can we revisit the fact that Adam and Eve were actual, living entities?"

The old man leaned back and folded his arms across his chest. "Look, I know it's a lot to take in."

"No shit!"

"But the fact is, Elohim created them on the Seraphim home world. Whether they were made fully formed or they were the result of millions of years of evolution isn't clear. But really, it's a bit beside the point, don't you think?"

The younger man leaned forward intensely. "You're telling me," he said through gritted teeth, "that you can verify this? That there is actual, quantifiable evidence of this Elohim? Of *God?*"

"I'd like to finish my story, if I may."

"But—"

"I'll get to the good stuff, I promise. Have a little patience."

The younger man sat back again and gestured to the recording device. "Proceed."

CHAPTER 12

"**H**ow close are we?" Alex asked. He twisted his hand around his M16, a new one that Hartinger had given him after he was well enough to move around.

"Three minutes away," Matthews replied.

Alex scowled. Kynlee had used all of the authority she could muster to keep Alex immobile as long as possible, but once he could walk, he called for Matthews and Hartinger to meet with him.

"I'm going to rescue Kate," he had told them, and watched as they exchanged tense looks.

"Shephard," Hartinger said, "that's suicide. No one's been able to infiltrate a harvesting camp. They're the most heavily guarded posts the Seraphim have. We'd be disintegrated by their lasers before we got within fifty feet."

"That's why we go stealth," Alex said. "You're both CIA. Blackest of the black ops. Don't tell me you don't know how to be invisible."

Matthews sighed. "Shephard—"

"I'm going, with or without you," Alex said. "That's nonnegotiable. Whether you come with me or not is up to you."

The two agents looked at each other again and seemed to communicate something silently. Then Matthews said, "Okay. I'm in." Hartinger just nodded.

And so there they were, two days later, a trio of heavily armed human beings about to attempt the unthinkable. The Seraphim and Malakhim had caused human beings to rethink all of their conceptions about angels and heaven, and now Alex and his companions were about to march straight into hell.

"Two minutes," Matthews said, pulling Alex out of his reverie. "We should be able to see the harvesting camp as soon as we turn this curve . . . oh, fuck."

Alex, seated in the backseat, craned to see. "*What?*"

"Shit," Hartinger said.

Then Alex saw it, about a mile ahead of them down the road. It was a huge building that must have been a factory before it was seized and turned by the Seraphim into a blood harvesting camp. Or rather, it *had* been a huge building.

It was a ruin now, and what parts of the building were left were still on fire, the thick black smoke winding its way into the night air. Jagged bits of metal and concrete rose out of the ground like teeth, a pale shadow of the building that had once stood there. Matthews brought the car to a stop, and the three men sat there, looking at the decimated structure, silent.

Then a soft growl began in Alex's throat. "No," he said.

Hartinger twisted around in his seat to look at him. "Shephard . . . I'm . . . I'm so . . ."

"No!"

Alex opened the car door, ignoring the sounds of Matthews' and Hartinger's voices calling out to him. He raced toward the burning structure. He ran maybe thirty feet before his legs gave out from under him, and he fell to his hands and knees, screaming.

This can't be happening.

Hoffman. Chan. Vasquez.

And now Kate. And our child.

He screamed until his throat was raw. He felt the very air itself choking him. He was vaguely aware of Matthews and Hartinger stood next to him, but it was like he wasn't living in the same world.

"Kate," he mumbled, his voice raspy and weak.

"She's gone, Shephard," one of them said. Alex couldn't tell who. "My God, I'm so sorry, but . . . she's gone."

* * *

The drive back to the cabin felt like it was happening to someone else. Alex listened, numb, as Hartinger told him that the firefights between the Seraphim and the newly rebelling Malakhim, as well as human insurgents who were gaining ground, often chose the harvesting camps as their targets.

Their plan was now to head to the base across the border in Canada and hole up there where they would be safe. "Or at least as safe as we can hope to be," Matthews said grimly. "We thought Hood would be safe."

"That we did," Hartinger said, nodding.

"Let's do it," Alex said. These were the first words he'd spoken since seeing the destroyed camp.

"What?"

"Let's go to Canada. I've lost everything. My friends. My fiancée. My unborn child. I've got nothing left that the Seraphim bastards can take from me. Let's gang up with our compatriots and unleash hell."

Matthews and Hartinger exchanged glances.

"Oorah," Hartinger said.

PART THREE

GOLGOTHA

CHAPTER 13

When they arrived, the base was a flurry of activity. Armed soldiers marched back and forth, and a team of scientists ran from one part of the main entrance room to another. The drive to the Canadian base had felt dark, cold, and isolated, so the explosion of sudden activity was an assault to Alex's senses.

Alex had ridden up with Hartinger, Matthews, and Kynlee. The three of them talked quite a bit, but Alex remained silent. It would seem that Matthews and Hartinger, who had spent so long in isolation, were making up for lost time in terms of human interaction, and both seemed quite interested in Kynlee. It turned out that she was a former military doctor who had entered the private sector after she was honorably discharged, devoting her time to researching, of all things, "theoretical biology of foreign bodies." In other words, the possible biology of extraterrestrials.

"Kind of a coincidence, isn't it?" Matthews said.

"Or not," Kynlee said.

"Meaning?"

"Come on, Matthews. You know as well as I do Uncle Sam has been privy to the existence of extraterrestrial life since '47."

"So it really was the Roswell incident that started this whole shebang, huh?" Hartinger said.

"Everyone should have listened to the nutcases all along," Kynlee said, smirking.

On hearing this, Alex had folded his arms and tried to sleep, but sleep wouldn't come. He tried not to picture Kate's final moments, but he couldn't help it. A kaleidoscope of images wheeled through his brain—Kate hooked up to tubes, her face pale from loss of blood, an explosion searing through the room.

He wondered if he would ever sleep again.

After they met with a crew of commanders who were in charge of the base, Alex was assigned a room. A young female Israeli soldier escorted him there, and on the way, Alex couldn't help but notice that human beings representing all the corners of the earth walked around them. A rainbow coalition of all the world's nations.

At long last, humanity had become united for a single cause. "The pale blue dot," he murmured.

"I'm sorry?" the soldier, whose last name was Levin, said.

"It was an old piece by Carl Sagan," Alex said. "There was a photo of the earth taken from Voyager, which showed the planet as this tiny pixel among the vastness of space. Sagan wrote a book about it, called it

Pale Blue Dot. Talked about how the entirety of human history happened on that one tiny speck. He pointed out how ridiculous it is that we fight against each other, given the size of us compared to the universe."

"Maybe we won't fight so much anymore," Levin said.

Alex looked at her. She was young—young enough to be an idealist, even while serving in the military. Even when facing the end of the world itself.

"Maybe," Alex said. He thanked her and stepped into his room, where he knew he would still not be able to sleep.

* * *

The next morning, Alex was eating in the mess hall when Matthews sat across the table from him. "There's a briefing at 1200 hours," he said without preamble. "I think you should be there."

"Briefing for what?"

"A mission. That's all I know now. But it's something big."

Alex studied Matthews' face, but of course the man chosen by the highest seats in government to guard its most important secrets gave nothing away. "Okay," Alex said. "Whatever it is, I'm in."

"Why don't you hold off on any commitment until we hear what it is?"

Alex shrugged and continued eating his food.

When the briefing time came, he followed Matthews through a series of hallways. Unlike the cavernous spaces of the secret base under Fort Hood, which allowed for a lot of breathing room, this base was more labyrinthine and claustrophobic, like some giant burrowing animal had just dug into the earth, carved a series of tunnels, and abandoned them. Alex hoped whatever the mission was, it would take him offsite.

They arrived in the briefing room, and Alex stopped in the doorway, frozen with a sudden rage. Looming over the humans stood what was undoubtedly a Seraphim, complete with its jet pack strapped to its back. Alex instinctively gripped the hold of his sidearm.

"Stand down," Matthews said quietly.

"What . . . the *fuck* . . . is this?" Alex said through clenched teeth.

"I told you there were friendly Seraphim here," Matthews whispered. "This one's on our side."

"I don't believe this."

Matthews took Alex out of the doorway and into the hall, where he gripped him by the shoulders. "Alex," he said. "That isn't the one who took Kate. He's different. Plenty of them are different. He has intel he wants to give us that will help in the fight. *Against his own people.* Remember that."

Alex forced himself to take a deep breath, then slowly nodded. When they reentered the room, he found it almost impossible to look up at the alien's face. But it was clear from the way the human scientists and military personnel were standing in a semicircle and facing him that the Seraphim was actually going to lead the briefing.

Unbelievable.

"Is everyone here?" a woman asked, and Alex realized it was Kynlee, who stood at a large monitor. When a military officer voiced the affirmative, she switched on the monitor, which displayed a picture of space. There was a star surrounded by four planets, and from their size Alex could tell it was not their own solar system.

The Seraphim pointed to the second planet out from the star. "This is Gan Eden," he said, and Alex fought a wave of nausea from hearing the alien speaking English. "It is my home world."

The humans in the room looked at one another.

"It has been explained to me that 'Eden' has a particular significance among your people. That the Seraphim who first came to your planet delivered our stories to you, and that they were adopted by humankind. But these tales have taken the form of mythology for most of you, religion. I understand it might feel odd to know that they were a literal fact."

"Almost," Alex muttered.

The Seraphim looked out at the humans in front of him, and Alex was shocked by what he saw: there was a look of consternation on the alien's face. It was the first evidence of emotion he had ever seen a Seraphim display, and it was then that he started to realize the truth of Matthews' words to him. All of the Seraphim he had encountered up until that moment had been soldiers, hardened by battle, most likely trained to act like robots.

God knows I've seen enough human soldiers behave the same way, he thought.

But this Seraphim was different. He looked . . . sad.

"Though our Creator is in Ein Sof and we cannot speak to his desires, it is my belief he would not have wanted this from his children. And we are *all* his children," the Seraphim said. "Seraphim. Malakhim. And humans. This is why I am betraying my own people to help you. We are all one under Elohim."

"We appreciate the sentiment, Gavreel," Kynlee said.

Gavreel, Alex thought. He vaguely remembered the name from a book of angels his mother had kept.

Gavreel bowed slowly to her, then addressed the rest of them. "And now to our purpose," he said. "Gan Eden is many light years from Earth, and though we have the capability to fly here on a planet-to-planet voyage, long ago our scientists discovered that there is, in fact, a faster path. Much faster. It is my understanding that your scientists have already begun their studies of wormholes."

A buzz emerged as people whispered to each other.

A scientist raised his hand. "Excuse me, uh . . . sir," he said, clearly not sure how to address the alien. "I'm a theoretical physicist, and just to clarify, we have ideas, theories, about wormholes, but our species has yet to actually observe one."

"That's actually incorrect," a man in a British military uniform said. "At this point, the time for keeping governmental secrets is long past. As it happens, a coalition of several countries has been working together on a joint space program for almost as long as NASA has existed. The purpose was to explore the possibility of colonization of planets in other solar systems should Earth ever become inhospitable to human life. We sent out a craft over a decade ago that did, in fact, locate and track a wormhole."

Alex threw his hands in the air. He was getting a little tired of learning about all the ways his own government had deceived him.

"Were our theories correct?" the scientist asked.

"For the most part," the British official said. "I'm not a physicist myself, but as I understand it a wormhole truly does bend space-time and allow great distances to be traversed almost instantaneously."

There was more murmuring from around the room, and Alex shook his head. Even given the fact that the planet had been invaded by, not one but two, alien species, both of which were connected to the earliest beginnings of man's major religions, the idea of wormholes almost defied belief.

"Your analysis is correct," Gavreel said to the officer. "Wormholes are exactly that. A 'shortcut,' I believe your people call it. They are Elohim's greatest gift to us in terms of interstellar travel. And while they do occur in nature, they can also be fabricated. It is an extraordinary undertaking, but it can be done."

"Thank you, Gavreel," another man, this one in a Canadian military uniform, said. He stepped away from the crowd and stood next to the alien, who dwarfed him by two feet at least. The soldier said, "For those of you who don't know me, I'm Brigadier General Augustin. To bring everyone up to speed—no pun intended—Gavreel has already set to work constructing a wormhole."

Alex looked up, surprised.

"Where?" someone asked.

"In this very base, son."

A collective shocked gasp emerge.

"*Here?*" Alex asked.

"For those that are worried, I can assure you there is no danger," Gavreel said. "My people have long ago mastered the art of constructing a stable wormhole."

No one seemed too convinced, but Augustin plowed on anyway. "There is a mission of grave importance that is only possible because of the help that Gavreel and several of his compatriots have given us, not to mention our Malakhim allies as well. You are all called here because you represent the best of the best: those who have survived repeated attacks from a far superior enemy."

Alex shook his head. *Best of the best* was the last phrase he'd use to describe himself. Every single one of his comrades in arms had fallen, and he hadn't even been able to keep Kate alive.

Hartinger raised his hand. "Sir, if I may ask, what is the mission?"

Augustin looked over all of them gravely. "We intend to send a covert team through the wormhole to Gan Eden, the Seraphim home world."

This time there was no murmuring among the humans. Just shocked silence.

"Our bodies are dependent on new blood to survive," Gavreel explained. "Ever since we became this way, the harvesting of blood became our people's primary focus. But nature didn't always work with us.

"Occasionally, disease would occur, and blood would be corrupted. When this happened, quarantine was absolutely paramount. The worst of these blood diseases has been isolated by our scientists, in a laboratory on our planet. It is especially dangerous because it is so highly transmittable. If someone comes into contact with the blood, it can be absorbed through any mucus membrane or microscopic cut on the dermis."

"So it's not airborne?" Kynlee asked.

"No," Gavreel said. "There must be blood contact for it to be transmitted. The most perilous aspect of all is that it does not show any signs of its presence for days, sometimes weeks. If the infected are ignorant to their condition, they can infect many others before symptoms manifest."

"The plan is, we go in and we get the virus. But here's where it gets sticky. Our mission requires one person to infect him or herself," Augustin said. "We then make sure we get that individual's blood close enough to the Seraphim to infect them all."

"But sir," a younger soldier in the crowd said, "even if we were able to bring it back, the Seraphim still have airstrikes, bots, all sorts of offense. There's no way to know if this would be successful, even if we do weaponize the blood somehow."

Augustin frowned and looked as many of them in the eye as he could. "I'm not going to sugarcoat the next part of our plan. We don't intend to weaponize the blood. This is a simpler approach. Apparently at the blood harvesting camps, they clone all the blood cells they collect and store the majority of the usable blood on their ships. If the human being infected with this virus were taken to one of the camps, the virus would spread like wildfire, both here on the ground and in their aircraft. It would be a fatal blow to their military arm."

"A Trojan horse," Alex said.

Augustin turned to him. "Exactly," the man said. "In other words, this mission requires the most absolute of sacrifices—one's life for all of humanity. Needless to say, this mission is probably the most dangerous mission anyone on planet Earth has ever undertaken. We know we can breathe the air, as Gan Eden has an atmosphere virtually identical to Earth's. And we will have Seraphim guides. But remember—this is a mission to an inhabited alien planet. We simply have no precedent for this kind of operation, so everything will need to happen on the fly. And for those that go, you will have the weight of literally saving the world, and all of mankind, on your shoulders. So all we need now . . . are volunteers."

Every hand in the room shot up at the same time.

CHAPTER 14

Alex stood in front of the mirror in his tiny quarters and took off his shirt. He looked at all the scars that crisscrossed his body, a tome written in injured tissue of all the struggles he'd been through. About half of the scars had been acquired from his rough childhood scrapping with the other boys in his neighborhood, followed by four years of college football and ROTC, before basic combat training had made him a marine.

The rest were all Seraphim.

He considered himself one of the lucky ones—a marine who hadn't known actual combat, despite the wars going on. He was always ready, mentally prepared to go to Iraq or Afghanistan, or wherever the hell else fate decided was in store for him. But he'd never been deployed, and so he thought he just might get out in one piece, not be traumatized by the horrors of war, and end up being able to be a good a husband to Kate and a good dad to their eventual kids.

But war had come to them. Not from the east, but from the stars themselves. And now, after months of battle, he was on the eve of his first actual deployment.

A contingent of seventeen humans and three Seraphim, Gavreel being one of them, were going to be deployed. Hartinger and Matthews were coming, even though the higher-ups wanted them to stay closer to home. But they had told them, in the politest way possible, to go fuck themselves. They'd been through so much with Alex, and they weren't about to let him have all the fun.

He lay down on the bunk and tried to drift off. For the first time in as long as he could remember, he actually fell asleep and slumbered through the night. Eight whole hours of uninterrupted sleep. He may have been forced to redefine his idea of God, but that was surely a blessing.

He showered and dressed in his uniform, taking extra-long to tie his boots, to make sure he was 100% regulation. After all, he was about to represent the entire human race. He might as well look his best.

He joined the rest of the human members of the squad in the mess hall. He was curious that he had never seen any of the aliens ever eating, and said so. "They don't eat," Matthews said. "Their bodies process matter by absorbing its energy through touch, kind of like a form of osmosis. It's . . . weird to watch."

"Sorry I said anything," Alex said, shoveling a forkfull of eggs in his mouth.

"I wonder if they have sex?" one of the others said.

"They have sex." Kynlee, who just sat down to join them, said. "Much in the same way we do, actually. I guess the classics never go out of style."

"Dr. Kynlee," Alex said, nodding. "You joining us on a trip down the rabbit hole?"

"*Worm*hole, and no, I don't think so," she said. "I finished Basic more years ago than I care to admit and haven't touched a weapon since."

"You might be missing out. Could be fun," Hartinger said.

"Bring me back a postcard."

Alex laughed. This was typical military behavior—cracking jokes in the face of mortal danger. It was the way they were trained to handle these kinds of situations. Although he had to admit, this specific situation was pretty unique, to say the least. None of the old rules seemed to apply anymore.

"Well," Hartinger said, "it's just about time that Augustin wanted us to convene in the north wing lab. Everyone ready?"

"Oorah!" the marines shouted as one.

Hartinger nodded and rose, and the others followed his lead. Alex fell into step beside Hartinger as they headed toward the lab.

"Is it safe to assume you're taking point on this mission, sir?" he asked.

"Unless you have an objection."

Alex smiled. "No, sir, I do not. If someone's going to lead us, I'm sure as hell glad it's a Green Beret."

"Stop, you'll make me blush." Hartinger looked over at him. "Listen, Shephard, not to get all shrink on you, but . . . you sure you really want to do this?"

Alex looked at him. "Are you kidding? A chance to save the world?"

"With a high risk of mortality. I know you've been through the ringer, more than most of us. Are you sure you're in the right head space?"

Alex nodded. "I understand your apprehension. But this is all I've got left, sir. My duty to my country, and . . . my planet, I guess. And if it's all right with you, I'd like to volunteer to be the one to get infected."

Hartinger stopped walking, and Alex did as well. Hartinger addressed the others. "Everyone, head to the lab. We'll meet you there."

When they were gone, Hartinger put a hand on Alex's shoulder. "Are you absolutely sure you want to do this?"

"Kate's dead. My unborn baby. All my friends. I've given it a lot of thought, sir. If there is an afterlife, I'm okay with going there, because it means I'll get to see them—I'll get to see *her*—again. That makes it more than worth it to me."

"Goddamn, son," Hartinger said.

"So do I have your approval?"

Hartinger crossed his arms against his chest. "In Special Forces we were much more likely to be the ones ordered to our deaths than to be the ones doing the ordering. Can't say I particularly like how this feels."

"But you'll give it the okay?"

Hartinger thought for a moment, then nodded. "Yeah. I'll give it the okay. If you're really sure."

"I am."

"All right, then. Let's go teleport to another planet and get you infected with an alien virus."

"When you put it that way, it almost sounds fun."

"Guess we'll see."

They walked together to the lab, where Gavreel and two other Seraphim stood towering above the humans, each covered head to toe with lean muscle, bulging as though it were carved from stone. Alex looked in awe at the far side of the room. Erected against the wall was a ring-shaped metal construct almost as high as the ceiling, and within the ring was something that Alex had never seen before—a pale white substance that looked like liquid but crackled as though it were electric, hovering in the air, seemingly defying the laws of physics. Lined up along the adjoining wall were small two-man aircrafts, which Alex deduced were the vessels they'd be taking through the wormhole.

"So that's the star gate, huh?" he asked, and Hartinger laughed.

"Yup."

Matthews came to their side, and the three men just stood there for a moment, staring at the impossible object in front of them.

"Well," Matthews said, "what do you say we get this party started?"

"Sounds like a plan," Hartinger said.

He walked to the front of the crowd and turned to face everyone.

"Gentlemen," he said, looking each of them in the eye in turn, "I'm a former Green Beret who lived in isolation for the better part of the last decade, so suffice it to say I'm not exactly a great speech-giver. I don't have the words to describe what we're about to do, except to call it what it is: a mission unlike anything experienced by any member of the human race. Ever. In the totality of our history."

He pointed behind him towards the wormhole. "We go through that doorway, and we emerge on another inhabited world. No matter how much intel we have, no matter how much we know what's going in, nothing can truly prepare any of us for what we're about to do. But courage and grit and brass fucking balls in the face of unimaginable odds are defining characteristics of our species."

"Fuck yeah, they are!" one of the marines called out, and this statement was met with hollers of agreement.

Hartinger smiled. "Our ancestors were the kinds of men who moved mountains and battled the legions of hell to protect their own, and because of their bravery we're here today. Let's make 'em proud, and carry on that tradition. When we go through that doorway, we act as a team and we get our mission done. Because I believe that when we put our minds to it, there isn't one goddamn thing on this earth or beyond we can't accomplish. So what do you say we go make history?"

Shouts of "Oorah" thundered up from the room. Alex turned to Matthews, who clapped him on the shoulder. "Let's get it done," he said, and Alex nodded.

* * *

It was time. Alex climbed into one of the craft and was joined by Hartinger. The vehicle was about half the size of a sedan, a cold metal construct with foam rubber seating. There were three sets of seat belts, and they were all instructed to strap themselves in as tightly as possible, which Alex was more than happy to do.

"Think there'll be turbulence?" he asked, trying to make a joke.

"According to Gavreel, it's a smooth ride. The belts are just in case something goes wrong."

Alex gulped. "What could go wrong?"

Hartinger shrugged. "We're about to take space and bend it like a pipe cleaner. Seems to me there's a likely margin for error."

"Oh, good. That's encouraging."

The crafts were set to autopilot and would move on their own once the lead craft—the one holding Alex and Hartinger—started its motion. When all the men were strapped in, Hartinger hit the big red button on his dash, and the craft lurched forward, rolling toward the ring-shaped construct.

"Holy shit," Alex whispered. "This is really happening."

"When we get out of this craft, we're going to be stepping onto a different planet," Hartinger said, then hollered like a cowboy in a rodeo. "Take that, Neil Armstrong!"

A wave of nausea hit Alex, and he swallowed hard and did his best to ride it out. Hartinger's joviality wasn't making him feel any less nervous about what they were moments away from doing. He tried to slow his breathing, to decelerate his heartbeat, to do anything he could to calm himself down. But nothing was working, and as the craft crept forward, he knew it was pointless to try.

The nose of their craft hit the odd liquid-like matter that swirled within the metal ring. What happened next was a sensation the likes of which Alex had never experienced before. It felt as though he was being stretched and turned inside out all at once. Everything went white—he felt weightless. Even worse, he felt *massless*, like he no longer existed inside his own body. Sound and vision ceased to be. Then suddenly it was over, and he was restored, like a rubber band being pulled to its maximum length and finally snapped back to its original form.

He took a few breaths and felt like he was going to vomit but suppressed the instinct. He realized his eyes were closed, and so, tentatively, he opened them.

"Son of a bitch," he breathed as he looked through the window of the craft.

The first thing he noticed were trees—pine trees. And beyond that, a clear blue sky.

"We're still on Earth," he said.

"How do you figure?" Hartinger said.

Alex pointed to the pine trees.

"You really haven't been paying attention, have you?" Hartinger said, chuckling. "Where do you think our trees came from? Remember, the Seraphim took flora and fauna from their world and planted their genetic seeds on Earth. Did the same thing with the Malakhim home world."

"God. Was anything just . . . ours?"

Hartinger thought for a minute. "Probably the platypus. No way that happened by intelligent design." Hartinger placed a finger on the button that would open the craft. "You ready to take your first breath of alien air?"

Alex shifted uncomfortably. "What are the odds we can't actually breathe the air? You don't think our heads are gonna swell up and pop like balloons, do you?"

Hartinger shrugged. "One way to find out." He hit the button, and the craft's roof sprang back.

Alex took a deep breath. "Well, not exploding yet."

"I'd call that a win."

Slowly Alex pulled himself out of the craft and looked around to see his fellow pioneers doing the same, with Gavreel and the other two Seraphim towering above them. They were in a clearing in the middle of a pine forest, which looked to Alex like any pine forest in the eastern United States.

Can we really be on another planet? he wondered.

But then, a small animal scurried by the men, and a few of them jumped in alarm. The creature was about the size of a rabbit and furry but had a long tail and mouse-like ears. It ran away from the men, then launched itself into the air and glided on fleshy wings, like a flying squirrel, beating the air behind it with its tail.

"Are you fucking serious?" one of the soldiers whispered.

"Well, I guess we're not on Earth," Alex said. "But wait. I thought the Seraphim engineered our animals from their own? Whatever that thing was definitely does not exist on Earth."

Overhearing, Gavreel said, "You are correct." He approached Alex and Hartinger. "But our planet is home to many species we did not bring over."

Alex found he still couldn't look Gavreel in the eye. "Thanks for the explanation," he said brusquely. He turned to Hartinger. "What now, boss?"

"I'd say it's high time we got down to business," Hartinger said. "All right, men. Here we are. Through the looking glass. We all know our objective. Gavreel here is going to lead us to the Seraphim laboratory, with Netzach and Haniel serving as auxiliary guides and defense."

The other two Seraphim nodded their heads.

"Gavreel?" Hartinger said, gesturing to the Seraphim.

Gavreel nodded. "The craft will be too easily picked up by our sensors if we use their engines, so we will have to travel on foot to avoid detection. This forest extends for approximately five miles and ends at the border of our capital city, Golgotha."

Alex looked up in surprise. Golgotha, of course, was the site outside of Jerusalem where Christ had been crucified. Even though Alex now knew that all the major components of his religion were derived from Seraphim history, this shook him. So far, everything about the Seraphim—the names, the Garden of Eden, the angelic hierarchy—all came from the Old Testament.

But Golgotha was strictly New Testament. There was a part of Alex, buried so far down he didn't even realize it, that had clung to the hope that the story of Jesus would remain unmarred by the Seraphim's revelations. That the one perfect and holy person who had walked the earth so long ago was truly the Savior of Man. Not Seraphim, not Malakhim, but Man.

And now even that was taken from him.

The crew trudged silently along through the underbrush for about an hour, but then it seemed the wonder of a new world began to give way to tedium.

"This forest just looks exactly like Earth. Kinda wanted something different," a marine said to his left.

"Like what? Purple trees?" the marine's companion said.

"Anything, man. All these pine trees just look like the woods I grew up near in New Jersey."

"Then this truly is hell."

Despite himself, Alex cracked a smile. But just then, Gavreel fell into step beside him, and his smile vanished. "There something I can help you with?" he asked the alien without looking at him.

"Kevin Hartinger told me that you have volunteered to be infected with the blood virus," Gavreel said.

"S'right."

"That is very courageous."

"I guess."

Gavreel just nodded as they walked along. Frustrated, Alex asked, "What do you want? Why are you talking to me?"

Gavreel looked surprised. "I suppose I was curious to meet the human who is so willing to give his life to protect his species."

"Well, congrats. You met him."

"Self-sacrifice is a trait we have observed in humanity over the millennia. It has always interested us, for deeply encoded in our genes is the self-preservation technique."

Alex shrugged. "Guess that's what makes us human and you Seraphim. We know how to do what's right. Even if we have to pay the ultimate price."

Gavreel pondered that for a moment, then said, "Are you familiar with the human called Jesus?"

Alex squeezed his eyes closed. He couldn't handle having this talk, not with a Seraphim. He already knew the unbearable truth. He didn't need some eight-foot-tall freak telling him everything he had ever believed was wrong.

"It is a curious thing," Gavreel said. "Our records, passed down from the Ancient Ones, contain words exchanged with the Creator before he entered Ein Sof."

Alex finally turned and looked at Gavreel. His curiosity overcame him. After all, how many times would he have the opportunity to hear the literal words of God? "Ein Sof. That's his sleep, right?"

Gavreel smiled softly. "It is much, much more complicated than sleep. But I suppose that is the simplest way for a human to understand it."

"So . . . what did he say?"

"They make mention of . . . forgive me, it is hard to put into words. There is a . . . part of him, a piece of his essence, that he can send out, even when he is in Ein Sof. There is no explanation of how such a thing could happen, and it defies all of our science and understanding of the universe. Quite simply, it should be impossible."

"Where are you going with this?"

"Two thousand years ago, there was a contingent of Seraphim who were tasked with observing humanity's development. It was learned that there was a human named Jesus who committed acts that astounded and perplexed the Israelites. Thinking that perhaps this was an aberration in humanity's evolution, the Seraphim observed Jesus closely. One night, he walked into the wilderness of Judea, and the Seraphim followed. It was then that he revealed the truth: that he was Elohim, who had taken the form of man, even as his greater consciousness still slept on Gan Eden."

Alex just stared at Gavreel, not knowing what to say.

"The Seraphim were astounded," Gavreel went on, "but Elohim told them there was something special about humanity. He wished to protect mankind in a way he did not believe he needed to with the Seraphim, or even the Malakhim. Though he was not directly responsible for creating them, he felt that humans were . . . his children. The Seraphim argued with him, telling him that humankind was constructed only so that the Seraphim could prosper, but Elohim told them that humans had transcended their original purpose. Elohim . . . *loved* them. Again, the Seraphim argued, and this argument lasted—"

"Forty days and forty nights," Alex whispered.

"That is correct," Gavreel said.

"Forty days and forty nights in the desert, when Jesus was tempted by the Devil but strengthened by . . . by angels."

"That is how your people came to interpret this story now, yes."

"So . . . Jesus *was* real," Alex said.

"He was."

"But how do you know all this?" Alex asked.

"Because," Gavreel said, "I was there. I was part of the observation team. I sat with him in the desert for that time."

Alex just shook his head in wonder.

"As I said," Gavreel continued, "there is no explanation in our science for how the Creator could accomplish such a feat. And so the only conclusion we have been able to come to is that it is, quite simply . . . a miracle. It is that moment that moved me to go against my brethren and protect the human race."

Alex looked at Gavreel, awestruck.

"When Elohim was in human form, he chose to endure torment and death, because he loved humanity. And now you willingly do the same. No Seraphim in existence would make this choice, but you do. I believe that, too, is nothing short of miraculous."

Alex, not knowing quite what else to do, just nodded.

Gavreel was called by the other Seraphim, who announced that they would soon be reaching the edge of Golgotha, and so he gave Alex a slight bow and moved away. Alex continued walking, lost in his thoughts.

Gavreel had verified that, impossible as it seemed, given all he had learned over the recent past, Christ had not only walked the Earth, but was in fact God as Man. Unbidden, the memory of a conversation he'd had with Kate right after meeting with Amitiel for the first time flashed into his mind. He remembered her words to him: *I still have faith. I think maybe, just maybe, the Seraphim making us was part of God's plan. Maybe they were just the method that he used in order to get us here.*

She had been right, after all. She'd seen the truth in a way he couldn't.

Well, babe, he thought. *Despite all this shit, I know now that God is real. Jesus is real. That means heaven is real, too. I'll be seeing you soon.*

* * *

At last, they reached the edge of the forest and could see the capital city of Golgotha. It was there that the reality of the fact that they were no longer on Earth was truly made manifest. The city was a sparkling circle of crystalline towers that reached into the sky like a chandelier turned upside down. It seemed to grow from the ground itself, organically, and Alex found himself wondering if the structures within the city did in fact have some biotechnological connection to the Earth in the same way that the Seraphim were part organism and part machine.

The beauty of the city was awe-inspiring, and the men allowed themselves a few seconds to just stare and take it all in. But then their military training snapped right back on, and they all turned to Hartinger, awaiting orders.

"This is the plan, men," he said. "We wait until dark. Then Gavreel, Netzach, and Haniel will take point and scout the entrance. Once they give the all clear, we head inside in a tight double-line formation. The laboratory is about half a mile in from the city gates. We move quick and fast. Simple get-in-get-out mission. Gavreel will handle the actual transference of the virus into Shephard."

The men all turned and looked at Alex. He was never comfortable with being the object of attention, and he found himself wishing they would look away.

But then Matthews spoke. "We owe you a debt of gratitude, Shephard. So does the whole human race. And I think it's pretty fitting that you're making this sacrifice in a place called Golgotha. Couldn't be anything more Christlike than giving up your life for the lives of your fellow man."

"Goddamn right," one of the grunts said, which was followed by a chorus of agreement and *oorahs*.

Hartinger clapped Alex on the shoulder and nodded. Alex returned the nod, and said, "We're all risking our lives, sir. Every man here. Everyone deserves the same thanks."

Matthews nodded. "Well said."

It felt like hours before night fell, but finally the world around them grew dark. The city of Golgotha lit up against the sky in a fashion Alex had never seen before. A gentle glow emanated from the buildings as though they were covered with a translucent phosphorescent skin. No individual lights could be seen, but the city itself shimmered.

Silently, Gavreel and the other two friendly Seraphim moved out from the protection of the trees and approached the border of the city. As they neared the edge, Alex realized there was a bizarre sheen in the air right where the buildings met the grass, just a hint of light every now and then.

"It's a force field," Hartinger whispered. "No regular old walls for the Seraphim."

"Guess not," Alex said.

Gavreel produced a strange, wand-like object and drew a few circles in the air, and the shimmer dissipated in front of them, opening up in a schism about ten feet across. The Seraphim waved to them, and the humans silently followed, two by two, in a long line, snaking out from the trees, crossing the open threshold, and entering the city.

Alex was never one for sightseeing, but he found himself wishing that he could explore the roads and valleys of Golgotha. What amazed him was that, even despite the fact that it was clearly alien, there was something so familiar, so *standard* about it. First there were the high-rises, which seemed to be used for some official purposes, like government or commerce. These were then surrounded by smaller domed constructs, which seemed to be living spaces. Light-years from Earth, on an alien planet, and still, a city was . . . just a city.

This is so unreal, he thought.

The troop moved as silently as they could through the city streets, seventeen human men led by three alien giants. Soon they reached a large, oval-shaped building that looked like it was made out of polished white marble. When Gavreel slowed to a walk Alex knew this must be the laboratory.

He squared his shoulders and took a breath. He had meant it when he told Hartinger he was sure this was what he wanted to do. But it was one thing to accept your fate and another to actually go through with it.

He instinctively went to touch his cross and then remembered he had foolishly thrown it away after learning the truth of mankind's origin, and Kate had come to speak her soothing words to him. He shook his head sadly at his own impetuousness.

Forgive me, he said in a silent prayer. *I was wrong to despair. Grant me the strength now to do what must be done.*

Ever since his first talk with Amitiel, he had stopped praying. But now everything was different once again. Jesus had lived. True, it wasn't exactly as Alex had understood his life, but he had been real. And his existence even mystified the seemingly omniscient Seraphim to the point where they believed it was a miracle. If that didn't warrant a little prayer, he didn't know what did.

Gavreel and the other Seraphim hovered around a space on the outside wall, and Alex realized it was a door. He had to look closely to see a slight outline where the door opened, for it was almost perfectly smooth against the wall. After a few minutes, they murmured to one another and stepped back, and the area where the door was simply dissolved into nothing.

"That's some crazy tech," Hartinger said.

"We could use something like that on Earth," Matthews said. "Imagine how easily security could be enforced."

"Make sure to take notes," Hartinger joked, and they all moved inside, urged on by their Seraphim guides.

The interior of the laboratory was a garishly bright white. Everything—from the walls to the instruments—seemed to have been bled of all color. Alex looked around at the humans in their dark military gear, sticking out like a sore thumb against the snowy backdrop. If they were discovered, finding cover would be impossible.

"Let's do this fast," he said, and Hartinger and Matthew nodded.

"Gavreel, can we move this along?" Hartinger said.

"Of course," Gavreel answered, and led the team to a section of the laboratory outfitted with large glass cylinders. He stood in front of one of them, and though it looked empty, Alex realized it was actually filled with a transparent liquid.

"Is that it?" he asked.

"This is the blood virus, yes," Gavreel said. "It will just take a few minutes to prepare the injection."

"Quick as you can," Hartinger said, and Gavreel set to work.

The other men created a perimeter, their weapons drawn in case there was any unwelcome company.

Matthews patted Alex on the arm. "I can't tell you how impressed I am, Shephard. You're a real hero. You know that?"

"I'm just happy to do what I can for the human race, sir."

Matthews' expression softened. "Kate . . . would have been mighty proud."

"Damn straight," Hartinger agreed.

Alex felt a lump form in his throat. He nodded stoically.

"Thank you," he said.

"I'm not . . . I'm not really sure what I should say," Hartinger said. "What you're doing is . . . so monumental. I feel like it should be commemorated. But I don't know what to say."

Alex thought about that. "I think sometimes, just being around is enough. You don't need to say anything. But if you want . . . if you're the kind of person who prays . . . a little prayer never hurt nobody."

Hartinger nodded.

"It is ready," Gavreel said.

He held in his hand a tiny needle with what looked like a bulb at the end—the Seraphim version of a syringe, Alex guessed.

Well, here we go, he thought.

He rolled up his sleeve and offered his arm to Gavreel, who took it. The needle slipped easily and painlessly into Alex's vein, and Gavreel held it in for one moment before removing it. There was the tiniest drop of blood on Alex's arm, and he saw the Seraphim nervously step away from it.

"I believe it would be best if you bandaged yourself," Gavreel said, and Alex heard fear in his voice for the first time. If the Seraphim were so afraid of this virus, that was a damn good sign for its use as a weapon.

Alex wrapped up his arm with a cloth that Gavreel indicated, and then turned to Hartinger and Matthews. "So, that was easy," he said.

"Great," Hartinger said. "Now all we got to do is skedaddle over to the—"

He was cut off by a sudden loud clanging that rung all through the laboratory. The lights inside quickly changed color, and what was once a snow-white environment was now bathed in a harsh blood-red light.

"We have been discovered!" Gavreel shouted.

"Fuck!" Hartinger said. "Men, line up! Defensive ring around Shephard!"

Alex armed himself and leaned toward Gavreel. "We have to get out of here!"

"Yes," Gavreel said, and Alex saw the air shimmer behind him—he was starting up his jet pack. "We do."

It was then that a swarm of Seraphim flew into view, and Alex cursed. There were even more than the attack on Fort Hood. They came like locusts, their blank white eyes wide, their expressions cold and somehow even more inhuman on their own planet.

"Open fire!" Hartinger yelled.

Alex and his companions quickly complied, and in seconds the air was ringing with the sound of bullets discharging, forming a counterpoint to the unsettling hum of the Seraphim's lasers.

"Get down! Find cover!" Hartinger ordered.

Alex felt a massive hand grab the back of his head and pull him down onto the ground. He looked in surprise and saw it was Gavreel. "What the hell are you doing?" he screamed.

"You must be kept safe," Gavreel said, staring at him blankly. "It is the priority of the mission."

"We have to fight them off!" Alex argued. "To keep everyone safe!"

"No," Gavreel said. "You are the priority. The lives of the others, including mine, are secondary."

"Bullshit!" Alex screamed, and stood and opened fire. He snared two Seraphim with head shots and watched as they careened down from the air and crashed into lab equipment.

But more hostiles were pouring in, and soon the air was thick with aliens.

"Gavreel!" Hartinger shouted. "Get Shephard out of here!"

"No, we all came together! That's how we're leaving!" Alex protested.

Hartinger picked off a Seraphim that was just feet away, and the giant body landed with a thud at their feet.

"Son," Hartinger said, "you're the last hope of the goddamn human race. We all knew when we took this trip we might not be coming back. But you have to—"

He never finished his sentence. A laser burst through his chest, carving a gruesome hole that immediately cauterized itself.

"No!" Alex shouted.

Matthews, who was fighting nearby, turned and saw Hartinger slump to the ground. "Hartinger!" he cried, and ran to his body. But anyone could see immediately there was nothing to be done. Hartinger was dead.

"Shephard!" Matthews said. "*Go!*"

Alex looked at all the men that had come with him on this journey. He couldn't just abandon them.

"But—"

Matthews gripped his arm. "Alex," he said quietly. "You need to let us go."

Alex looked in Matthews' eyes and saw the man meant it. He was prepared to die for the cause. They all were.

"Shit," he said.

"We'll see each other again," Matthews said. "On the other side."

Alex looked around frantically, and for a moment it seemed that time had slowed down. Bullets and beams of light danced through the air, accompanied by a chorus of buzzes from the Seraphim's wings. He saw men and aliens dying alike, grasping onto their companions in the last seconds of life before succumbing.

War is hell, William Tecumseh Sherman said during the Civil War. Alex remembered learning that in middle school, and it had stuck with him ever since. It was a phrase every military man knew.

And now Alex understood the truth of it. The other side of hell was heaven, and that's where he would soon be. He would be there with Hartinger. And Hoffman and Chan and Vasquez.

And Kate.

Always Kate.

He gripped Matthews' arm and nodded.

He felt giant arms close around him and knew that Gavreel was picking him up and planning to fly out of the laboratory with him. He let himself be lifted and watched with a kind of numb detachment as they soared through the battle.

His senses soon recovered, and he assisted Gavreel by picking off as many Seraphim in their path as he could with his firearm while Gavreel also delivered his deadly blasts. They cut through the horde of hostiles in a jagged swath, almost being sliced open by the Seraphim's laser fire more times than Alex could count.

Gavreel flew toward the door they entered from, but they were quickly cut off by a phalanx of Seraphim descending from above them.

"Bank left!" Alex screamed.

A Seraphim was suddenly on them, grasping at Alex. He wheeled his machine gun around and smashed the butt of it into the Seraphim's face. The alien crashed to the ground in a crunch of bones and muscle.

"This exit is blocked," Gavreel said grimly.

He pivoted around in the air and took off in another direction. Just as he did, Matthews came into Alex's view. He was battling a Seraphim on the ground with his bare hands. Somehow he had lost his weapon, and he was too close for his enemy's blast range. But the Seraphim was stronger, and Alex watched in horror as it snapped Matthews' neck.

"No!" Alex screamed.

He aimed his gun and took the Seraphim down.

It seemed impossible. Hartinger and Matthews, dead. Just like that. "Keep flying!" he yelled to Gavreel.

Gavreel did, and they broke through a haphazard line of Seraphim and away from the battle. Gavreel veered to the right, and they flew out a small window, just wide enough for them to both pass through without hitting the sides.

Alex felt sick, and he wasn't sure if the nausea was due to Gavreel's aerial feats or the sight of his companions' deaths. All he knew was they needed to get out.

This was war. And war *was* hell.

Gavreel took them at an almost unbearable speed, and Alex could tell they were not headed in the direction of their crafts. "Where are we going?" he asked.

"To another laboratory," Gavreel said. "One that is outfitted with the wormhole technology. We must get back to Earth if the mission is to be successful."

"No shit," Alex muttered.

They flew through the city, hiding when Gavreel detected Seraphim nearby, ducking into alleys and crevices between buildings. Soon Alex saw another building that looked from the exterior very much like the laboratory they had just left behind them.

"Is that it?" he asked.

"It is."

"Okay."

They reached the building and Gavreel landed, letting go his grip on Alex. Alex did his best to look dignified, but even holding an M16, he felt childish, having just been carried by a larger body.

Gavreel went to a panel that was positioned next to the door, and he entered an elaborate code, his fingers flying over the keypad. The door whooshed open, and Gavreel urged Alex inside. "Haste is paramount," he said.

"Again, no shit," Alex said as they rushed through the corridors.

The laboratory was set up differently than the one they had just come from. As opposed to the open layout of the first lab, this was more labyrinthine, with passageways and doors leading to who knows where. If it weren't for Gavreel's guidance, Alex would have been lost in a few seconds.

Soon they reached what seemed to Alex to be the center of the laboratory. There he saw a construct almost identical to the one Gavreel had set up in the base on

Earth, a craft much like the ones they had traveled with stood on the floor, facing the giant metal ring.

"How long till this thing can zap me home?" Alex asked.

Gavreel hit a button, and what looked like a keyboard made of light appeared out of thin air in front of him. "Several minutes," he said, typing furiously.

"Let's hope we don't have company," Alex said. He gripped his gun.

Just then, he heard a sound in the distance. The hum of the Seraphim's jet packs.

"Why the hell did I say that out loud?" Alex asked miserably.

"I will continue programming," Gavreel said. "You will need to do whatever you can to keep them at bay."

"Copy that," Alex said, raising the gun.

The sounds of the Seraphim getting closer increased. Palms sweaty, Alex held the gun as still as he could.

Despite himself, he found that he was praying. To God. To Jesus. To Mary. His faith had carried him this far, and even when he deserted it, it was still there for him. *Deep breath,* he thought. *You're going to get home. For the others. For Kate. For the child you'll never know.*

A Seraphim appeared in the doorway, and Alex took it out with one shot right through the eyes. Another appeared behind it, and Alex dispatched that one with one shot as well.

"One more minute," Gavreel said, typing faster than Alex had ever seen anyone type before.

Three Seraphim hostiles came in a line, and Alex mowed them down, but four appeared behind them. "Not sure we have another minute!" Alex shouted.

He blasted that row of bogeys, but it was no good. More were soaring in and coming at them. Fast.

"Finished," Gavreel said.

Alex raised his gun again, but before he could fire he felt a large hand grab him from behind. Before he realized what was happening, Gavreel tossed him with one arm into the craft that would take him through the wormhole. The alien slammed the button on the dash down and backed away as the doors around Alex closed.

The craft lurched forward and crawled on autopilot toward the metal ring. Alex watched through the glass as Gavreel turned to face the oncoming horde. He was immediately decapitated by a beam from one of the encroaching Seraphim. Alex let out a shout, but there was nothing he could do. He watched in horror as Gavreel's headless body slumped over and fell to the ground. Alex realized the Seraphim had just become more human than he ever thought possible, sacrificing himself for the human race.

One of the aliens, ahead of his companions, crossed the distance to Alex's craft and seized it with its impossibly large hands. The craft shook, and for one horrifying moment Alex thought that all was lost, that the Seraphim would wrest the craft away from the wormhole and destroy all their hopes for the survival of the human race.

But then he felt a strange pull, as though his insides were stretching. He remembered this feeling from their journey over, and so he turned and looked around and realized the nose of his craft was already in the wormhole.

His journey home had begun.

The last thing he heard from the Seraphim was a hideous cry of outrage.

CHAPTER 15

"He's back!"

"Get him out of the shuttle!"

"Where are the others?"

"What happened over there?"

"Was the mission a success?"

"Shephard?"

"Shephard!"

Alex was vaguely aware of the sound of voices. At first they seemed like a constant buzzing, like a chorus of cicadas. Eventually, they coalesced into recognizable language. He started to recognize his own name.

"Shephard?"

"Come on, Marine. Nod if you can understand me."

Alex couldn't feel his body at first, and he thought maybe he had lost form somehow in the wormhole, and was no longer bound to an earthly body.

Then he felt someone poke him sharply in the chest, and he dismissed that theory. *I've been hanging around too many aliens,* he thought to himself. "I hear ya. Back off," he murmured.

There was a buzz around him, and he realized he was surrounded by people, but he couldn't see anyone.

Have I gone blind?

Oh, he realized. *My eyes are closed.* Slowly, cautiously, he opened one eye and looked around.

Okay. Progress. He opened the other eye.

"Nice seeing those pretty eyes again, Marine," someone said.

Dr. Kynlee, Alex realized. "Wish I could say the same," Alex muttered. The crowd of people around him laughed.

"How are you feeling?" Kynlee asked.

"Like my body was just stretched through a toilet paper tube."

"Huh," Kynlee said, looking thoughtful. "That's actually not that inaccurate a representation of what happened to you."

"Fantastic."

"I mean when you went through the wormhole."

"Yeah, I got it, Doc."

Groggily, he sat up and looked around. He was on a cot in the medical bay. There was a crowd of medical and military personnel standing there, staring at him.

"Hi," he said.

There was a series of nods and a few soft *hellos.*

"Shephard," Kynlee said, "everyone here is, as you can imagine, pretty damn invested in your well-being. We just wanted to make sure you were okay."

"What happened?"

"After you came through the wormhole, you were unconscious."

Alex thought hard for a moment.

"I don't get it," he said.

"What?"

"When I went through the first time, I was fine. I didn't pass out. Didn't even feel lightheaded."

"Well, the last time you went through, your body wasn't playing host to an alien blood virus."

Alex scratched his head. "I guess that's a good point."

"Your vitals are good, all things considered. Your insulin levels are a little unusual, and you seem to have hypoglycemic symptoms all of a sudden, which definitely weren't present before you left."

"That because of the virus?"

"That would be my guess, yes."

"I don't feel any different."

"Well, that's good."

An older man stepped toward Alex from the group, and Alex realized it was Brigadier General Augustin. "Welcome back, Shephard," he said.

"Thank you, sir."

The general extended his hand, and Alex shook it. "I just wanted to shake the hand of the man who's making the ultimate sacrifice for his fellow man," Augustin said.

Alex sighed. "All due respect, sir, I'm getting tired of hearing that."

"Sorry?"

"We all made the sacrifice. I lost a lot of friends along the way, all of them fighting to stay alive. And the rest of our contingent who went to Gan Eden all died so I could deliver the blood virus into the Seraphim camps. I'm not special."

Augustin nodded slowly. "You're a good man, son," he said. "But give yourself some credit. You're very special."

Alex didn't know how to respond to that, so he simply looked away.

"All right, everyone, you've seen him and talked to him. Now we need to let Alex rest," Kynlee said.

"Shouldn't I just head out?" Alex said.

"Excuse me?"

"Get captured. Isn't that the plan? Why wait?"

"You'll need to be medically cleared first. I want to make sure you actually make it to the Seraphim camp. You'll be of no use to anyone if you keel over before you get the chance to sacrifice yourself."

Alex nodded, and Kynlee looked around at everyone. "I mean it. Out!"

The crowd dispersed and shuffled out of the room. Kynlee put a hand on Alex's shoulder. "Get some rest," she said.

Alex sighed and sank back down onto the cot.

* * *

He woke several hours later. He looked around and realized he was alone. *Always alone from here on out,* he thought.

In the dark of the medical bay, his thoughts drifted from face to face of the friends he'd lost. But of course, it was Kate's face that stayed with him the whole time. He'd never gotten to see her belly grow with their child inside of her. Never got to see her glow with the expectation of holding their baby. Never got to sit on the hospital bed with her as they looked down at their little miracle for the first time.

Tears came to him then, leaking out the sides of his eyes and spilling down his temples.

Miracle.

The Seraphim called Elohim's life as Jesus a miracle.

With all their science, all their understanding of the physical universe, they had no explanation of how such a thing was possible.

Because it wasn't possible. And yet it happened.

It had been a miracle.

In a time when the world was ending, when humanity was on the brink of destruction, maybe the hope of miracles is all we have, Alex thought.

A light switched on far away, and Alex saw someone entering the room. The person was only in silhouette, and Alex saw it was too large to be Kynlee.

The figure approached him and soon came close enough for Alex to recognize him. Augustin.

The man was definitely a career military officer. He held himself with the kind of posture Alex had seen over and over again from the higher-ups throughout his time in the marines. Back straight, chest out, eyes perfectly level. Alex had often wondered if he would end up like that one day.

Now he'd never live to be old enough to find out.

"Hi there, Shephard," Augustin said.

"Sir," Alex said.

He struggled to sit up. Augustin patiently waited until Alex was sitting before addressing him again.

"You feeling better?"

"I am, sir."

"Good. Glad to hear it."

"What can I do for you, General?"

Augustin let out a deep sigh and grabbed a folding chair near Alex's cot. He sat down and looked Alex in the eye.

"We sent seventeen of our own to an alien planet, and only one returned. Normally that's not what I'd call a successful mission."

"I agree, sir."

"However, in this particular case, our paramount objective was accomplished."

"Yes, sir."

"The time when we'd go through debriefing after debriefing, and swim through rivers of paperwork, is long over. We're flying by the seat of our pants now. But I do want to go over one thing with you."

"What's that, sir?"

Augustin leaned forward intently. "You were on an alien planet, Shephard."

"Yes, sir."

"An *alien planet*."

"Yes, sir."

"So my question is . . . what was it like?"

Alex looked at Augustin, and saw on the man's face a blend of the spark of wonder and the consternation of rigidly controlled fear. It was understandable. Humanity had adjusted to invaders from beyond the stars, but they were only ever seen on our turf.

"It was . . . I hate to say it, General, but it was beautiful."

"Beautiful?"

"The Seraphim themselves were just as alien and just as vicious as they are here. We were chased by a gang of them. They took out everyone except me."

"What saved you?"

"Gavreel."

Silence hung in the air between them for a moment.

"A Seraphim saved you from his own kind?"

"Yes, sir."

"When the humans with you couldn't?"

"Yes, sir."

Augustin leaned back. "When the strength of your companions failed, an enemy turncoat rescued you. Wouldn't be the first time in history that happened, but it doesn't make it any less poetic."

"Poetic?"

"Sure."

Alex shrugged. "I guess, sir. Um . . . if I might ask . . ."

Augustin raised his eyebrows, inviting Alex to continue.

"What's all this about, General?"

Augustin crossed his arms over his chest. "Are you a God-fearing man, son?"

Alex slowly nodded.

"I always thought that was a strange expression, growing up, 'God-fearing.' I remember when I was a child in Sunday school. I had the nicest young lady teaching that class, and she would always tell us that God was love. Why would anyone be afraid of such a thing, you know?"

"Yes, sir. Thought the same myself, a lot."

"But with everything that's happened in the recent past, I'm ashamed to say I've lost my faith. I guess I just wanted to speak with you, to hear from someone who was there, that our place in the universe really is as insignificant as it's come to seem lately. I know it's foolish, but I wanted to hear it for myself."

Alex frowned. "Have you spoken to any of the aliens about their history?"

"I know they genetically engineered humanity. That we were bred for spare parts and evolved under their direction."

"But have you spoken to them further? About their own origin?"

"Can't say that I have."

Alex took a deep breath. "This is going to sound impossible, sir, but . . . it's all true. Everything we ever learned about God. I mean, it didn't happen *exactly* the way we picture it. There was an Adam and Eve, but they were on Gan Eden, not Earth. But everything—*everything*—was devised by God. Elohim. He even came here, to Earth, as Jesus."

Augustin's mouth fell open. "You're serious, aren't you?"

"Yes, sir."

Augustin shook his head. "Well, God damn."

"And Gavreel told me that Elohim . . . when he was here, as Jesus . . . he spoke to the Seraphim who were stationed here. They didn't know why he came to Earth. He said it was because . . . he loved us. We were his children."

A tremor moved Augustin's lower lip, and he bit down on it, but it didn't stop the tear that escaped his right eye. Augustin didn't say anything then, but he sat there for a long while with Alex in silence. Finally he stood and patted Alex on the arm.

"Thank you, son," he said, and then he was gone.

* * *

Alex drifted in and out of consciousness for what felt like days. At times, he would wake to find Kynlee bustling about the medical bay. Other times it was some of the personnel working under her. But mostly he was alone.

He found himself longing for the crucifix that once hung around his neck. He touched his chest where the familiar cold metal of the cross should have been, and thought of Kate. *I'll be seeing you soon, baby,* he thought. *On the other side.*

He heard a soft rumbling of voices from far away, and soon the sounds grew louder. His whole body tensed, preparing for the worst-case scenario—that they were under attack by the Seraphim. If he was killed here, they wouldn't take him to a harvesting camp, and they wouldn't remove his blood and infect their supplies.

All the hell he had been through would be for nothing.

But there was something about the voices that made him think this wasn't the case. There wasn't any panic, really, or calls to arms, from what he could discern. Just a lot of people, talking at once.

Someone, a man Alex had never seen before, came into the medical bay and calmly checked on a few machines without a trace of panic.

We're definitely not under attack, then, he thought.

"What's happening?" Alex asked.

The man looked up.

"Sorry?" he asked.

"What's going on out there?"

"Oh, our scouts found a bunch of human survivors out there. They hauled them back in. Most of them are okay. A few need medical attention, so I'm making sure we're ready for the ones that do."

"Where'd they come from?"

"One of the blood harvesting camps. From what I could piece together, a camp was attacked by Malakhim ships, and there was a big firefight between them and the Seraphim. The humans that were in the camp got free and escaped."

"Jesus."

"Yeah. They were definitely lucky."

"I'll say. Where was the camp?"

"Um . . . where did they say?" The man looked down, scratching his head. Then he snapped his fingers. "Oh, Texas. Not too far from the base at Fort Hood, they said."

Alex sat bolt upright. "*Fort Hood?*"

The man looked surprised at his sudden volume. "Yeah."

Alex threw the sheet off of him and tore out of the room.

"Hey!" the man shouted after him. "Are you okay to get out of bed?"

Alex didn't respond.

He sprinted through the hallways of the underground base, his heart pounding in his chest. Immediately, he was winded—surely this was due to the Seraphim virus in him. But he wouldn't stop moving.

He couldn't.

His thoughts flew through his head faster than his feet could carry him.

Texas.

Fort Hood.

A harvesting camp full of survivors.

Kate.

He knew the likelihood of the camp being the one she was taken to was remote. Even more remote was the possibility that she had survived this long, even if it *did* end up being the same camp. But he had to see for himself.

He followed the sounds of voices, and as he raced through the corridors and the voices grew louder, he urged his feet on, even as he felt his lungs burn with the exertion. He grew woozy and stopped for a moment, holding onto a nearby wall for support.

Keep going, a voice in his head urged him. *Don't stop.*

He pushed himself ever onward, and soon found himself in a cavernous hangar, where about eighty people were milling about. Some were military officials, but the rest were clearly the refugees. They were ragged, dirty, clinging to each other in small groups, fear in all their eyes.

Alex raced from cluster to cluster of people, desperately searching for Kate's face. Every face he saw was one he'd never seen before, person after person completely unknown to him.

He started to panic, but then he saw something. It was a woman, her back turned to him, hair the color of Kate's tied into a messy ponytail. He felt his breath catch in his throat, and he walked over to her. But when she turned around, it was a stranger's face he saw.

The woman moved past him, not even noticing him. Alex sank to his knees, his insides on fire.

He clutched his stomach and squeezed his eyes shut. He didn't know why he let himself believe the impossible could happen, that Kate might actually have survived the horror of the harvesting camp. But of course it couldn't be. She'd been gone too long, had spent too much time in the clutches of the Seraphim forces.

He fell forward and caught the floor with his hands. He gasped for air, desperately trying to fill his burning lungs, unsure whether the symptoms he experienced were from despair or the alien virus coursing through his bloodstream.

All he wanted now was for Kynlee to clear him as quickly as possible. He wanted out of the bunker, away from the survivors who had hope for a future he would never share. After all he'd been through, he didn't fear death or pain. But the waiting was unbearable, and he wanted to see it end.

"Alex?"

It was a small, quivering voice, barely audible among the din of the refugees' conversations. Alex thought he had imagined it.

"Alex?"

No, he hadn't imagined it. It was just a tiny thing, but it was definitely there, and it was most certainly a woman's voice.

He took a deep breath and opened his eyes, turning towards the voice.

"Alex!"

And there she was, like something out of a dream.

Kate.

He blinked rapidly, trying to clear his vision, to assure himself that what he was seeing was really there.

Her clothes were ripped and filthy. Her face was smudged with dirt, and her hair was tangled and messy.

He had never seen anything more beautiful in his entire life.

"Alex!" she yelled again.

She seemed frozen, as though she couldn't trust her own eyes, but then she shook herself and ran to him. Alex half-stood as she barreled into him, wrapping her arms around him. He clutched her to him ferociously, and they both wept.

"Oh, my God," she sobbed into his shoulder. "I can't believe it's you."

Alex just held her, unable to speak.

After a few moments, he pulled back and looked into her eyes. "I can't believe it either," he stammered. "I just can't."

"Oh, my God," she said, and caressed his cheek with her hand. "It's really you."

"I tried to find you," he croaked out.

She nodded.

"I didn't want to give up."

"I know you didn't, baby . . ."

"But I saw the camp . . . it was destroyed."

"Alex . . ."

"I would have taken them all on at the same time to save you."

"I know you would have."

"But you were gone . . . and I was so lost . . ."

"We're together now," she said, and held him close to her.

There were a million more things Alex wanted to say, but as he opened his mouth to speak, he passed out.

* * *

Alex woke up some time later only to discover that he was back in the medical bay. He immediately sat up. And regretted it right away. His head pounded. He rubbed his forehead and moaned. Soft hands touched his shoulder. He looked up and saw Kate, and behind her, frowning, was Kynlee.

"How do you feel?" Kate asked, her voice soft.

"I'm okay," he said, "just a little lightheaded."

"I could have told you that," Kynlee said. "Remember what I said about your hypoglycemia? That's why you passed out. You haven't eaten anything substantial in days. You need to take it easy."

"Okay, Doc."

"I mean it."

"I know."

"You won't be a very good sacrificial lamb if you don't live long enough—"

"*Doc!*" Alex shouted. "Please."

Kate looked from Kynlee to Alex, confused.

"What does she mean?" Kate asked.

Kynlee immediately realized her blunder and cleared her throat, embarrassed. "I should let you two talk," she said, and moved away.

"Alex?" Kate asked.

Alex reached out and grasped Kate's hand in his. "Baby," he said. He was about to tell her everything but then found he couldn't bear to, at least not right away. "We'll talk about me in a second. What happened to you? I was knocked out in the fight at Fort Hood and woke up a hundred miles away. But I went back for you, baby, I swear it. Me and Matthews and Hartinger. We went back. I was going to get you. But when we got to the harvesting camp, it had already been destroyed."

"God, that awful place," Kate whispered. Her eyes glazed over slightly, and Alex winced. He'd seen eyes like that before, in political prisoners newly freed, still haunted by the torment they had endured. He couldn't bear the fact that he was now seeing it in her eyes.

"We were captured," she said. "The Seraphim came for all of us. The ones that fought back were killed on the spot. The rest of us were thrown in cages."

"Sweet Jesus."

"There were so many of us. They brought us to the factory they'd converted into a harvesting camp. It was like nothing I can describe. Nothing I've ever seen before."

"Did they . . . did they take your blood?"

"No. They never got a chance."

"What happened?"

"Oh, God. I don't even know where to start. After we were brought in, they held us for a while. I don't know if it was days or weeks or what. It was impossible to tell, because we couldn't see the sun. All the windows were blocked off."

Alex shivered. He felt more enraged than anything, thinking of her going through these horrors.

"Then they started taking some of us. To be, you know . . . harvested. One of the people in the cage with me was a nurse who'd given me a checkup when we were in Fort Hood. She knew I was pregnant, and she told everyone else. They kept me hidden in the back so I would be taken last. Then one of the Seraphim came, and he started walking right at me, but she stepped in the way so he would take her instead. She was so brave. It was unbelievable."

Alex felt a lump form in his throat. He remembered Gavreel telling him that no Seraphim would sacrifice their own life for the lives of another, as self-preservation was their defining trait. Humanity, it seemed, while of course invested in their own well-being, didn't possess such a shortcoming.

"She was a hero," Alex said.

"Yeah," Kate said, her eyes misting over. "She was. After she was taken, that's when the Malakhim attacked. It was chaos. There were explosions everywhere. The cages caught on fire with us still in them. A Malakhim ship crashed through the wall, and its weapons were still firing. It blasted a hole in the side of our cage. That's how we got out."

Her lip quivered suddenly, recalling the memory. Alex squeezed her hand.

"Anyway," she said, wiping away a tear, "there were about sixty of us in all. We survived by scavenging for a few weeks before we were found by a few soldiers who had survived out in the wilderness. They had a radio, and that's how they heard about the base here. The soldiers hot-wired a bunch of cars, and we all drove up together. We were intercepted by a group of people who heard our calls on the radio."

"Our scouts," Alex said.

"Yeah."

"And," Alex said nervously, "the baby?"

Kate grinned, took his hand, and pulled it to her belly. After a moment, he felt a tiny movement from inside.

"Kicking like a soccer champ," she said. "He never stopped moving during the entire ordeal."

"He?"

Kate shrugged "Well, it's just a hunch."

Alex just shook his head in wonder as he felt his baby kick. "It's a miracle," he said.

"Actually, funny you should say that," Kate said. "When we got out of the camp, we went back to Fort Hood to see if there was anyone else there who might have survived. The fort was a shambles, but I was out in front of the entrance, and I found this."

She reached into her pocket and brought her hand out. Before Alex's stunned eyes, she unfolded her fingers and revealed his crucifix, still attached to its chain.

"My God," he said.

"This has to be a sign," Kate said. "I know you're having problems with your faith right now, but—"

"No, honey," Alex said. "Not really. Not anymore."

"What happened?"

"I'll be damned if that's not one hell of a long story," he said, smiling slightly. "But, Kate . . . there's something we need to talk about first."

"What?"

He tried to swallow and found his throat was raw and tight. "Baby . . . I . . . we all thought you were dead.

I didn't think there was anyone . . . any reason left for me to . . . stick around. So I . . . I . . ."

"Alex," Kate said slowly, her eyes wide. "What did you do?"

"Oh, God. How do I even explain? There was a mission. We went to . . . I know this sounds impossible, but we actually went through a wormhole and traveled to the Seraphim home world."

"*What?*"

"I know."

"That doesn't sound possible."

"I know. It still feels like it should be impossible. But it happened."

"What was the mission?"

"There's a virus that the Seraphim have isolated, sort of like how we've isolated yellow fever. It's incredibly fast working."

She just looked at him intensely, waiting for him to go on.

"The plan was to bring it back here," Alex said, "and then send it into the Seraphim camps. According to our Seraphim allies, they take all the blood and put it in one container, so the disease would spread immediately to their entire blood supply, killing them all. It's a Trojan horse."

"Okay," she said. "But how do you get the virus into their blood source if it's in a vial or something?"

"We can't," Alex said. "That's why we needed a human host. Someone to let themselves be taken into the harvesting camps."

Kate sat back suddenly, looking horrified. "And that's you?"

Alex couldn't meet her eyes. "I'm sorry, babe, but yeah. It is."

Kate turned away, shaking her head in shock. "But we just found each other again. Against unbelievable odds. This can't be happening."

Alex reached out for her. "Come here."

Slowly she slid onto the bed next to him, and he held her in silence for a few minutes. She was crying, but her tears were without sound. They just flowed from her eyes like a waterfall.

He smoothed her hair back away from her forehead. "I know this timing is terrible," he said. "And I know there's nothing in the world that will really make this easier. But I have to go, babe. I have to go."

"But . . ." Kate said, sniffing. "Can't you just give the virus to someone else? A transfusion? Why does it have to be you?"

"There's no cure. Even if I did give it to someone else, I'd still have it. And with the virus in me, I wouldn't last too long."

Kate looked around frantically, desperate for a solution she'd never find. "I can't believe this is happening." She leaned her face into his shoulder and sobbed. He held her close, rubbing his hand up and down her back as he always did when she needed to be soothed.

"I love you," she said.

"And you know I love you," he said. "Kate, when I thought I'd lost you and the baby, the world ending didn't even seem so bad in comparison. But knowing you made it . . . that you're going to make it . . . that's nothing short of miraculous."

They held each other tightly, and Alex pulled the sheet over both of them. He knew in the coming days and with the hell that awaited him, it was this moment he would come back to for comfort and strength.

The time for his mission was soon going to come. But for now, they were a family.

* * *

Alex walked down the road, alone. It was late afternoon, and the sun was beginning its sluggish descent toward the horizon. The clouds were a rich kaleidoscope of vibrant colors, and Alex was sure he'd never seen the sky look so beautiful.

Strange thoughts entered his mind. He found himself wishing more than anything that he could hear some of his favorite music one more time. Led Zeppelin. The Stones. The Doors. He wondered if Jim Morrison put on concerts in the afterlife.

Music was a relic of the world that had been, but he also knew it would come back one day. Mankind was, if nothing else, resilient, and once his mission was successful, the artists would return, writing songs and painting pictures commemorating the time the human race had almost gone extinct. He found comfort in that fact.

He walked a few more miles. Just as the sun was about to slip away for the night, he saw them coming toward him: two low-flying Seraphim ships, coasting over the land, slow and steady.

Gathering ships.

He stopped walking and waited for them to come to him. They were backlit by the dying sunlight, and they appeared as just shapes approaching him, silhouettes floating against the backdrop of the beautiful sky.

Let them come, he thought. *Let them take me. What I'm about to go through, I'm doing for my fellow man.*

I'm doing this for Hoffman, and Chan, and Vasquez, and Hartinger, and Matthews.

I'm even doing this for Gavreel, the enemy of my enemy who gave his life for mine, proving maybe there was more to the Seraphim than he thought.

But most of all, I'm doing this for Kate, and our child.

He held his hands up over his head. When the Seraphim emerged from the ship, he didn't struggle but allowed himself to be taken, his head held high, knowing the fate of the world was on his shoulders and knowing he had done what needed to be done.

EPILOGUE

YEAR: 2109

The old man and the younger man sat, looking at each other for some time, neither saying a word. Finally, the younger man inclined his head. "And?" he said.

The old man looked at him. "And what?"

"That's not the end of the story."

"Well, for all intents and purposes, it is. He let himself be captured, and the plan worked exactly as the human rebellion hoped it would. The blood was taken, cloned, and stored with the rest of their blood. It was disseminated among the Seraphim here on Earth, and those were the militant ones that were the most dangerous. Oh, sure, there were aggressive factions still on Gan Eden, but there were also plenty of dissenters. Furthermore, the Seraphim on Gan Eden who were still intent on harvesting our blood realized that mankind was hardly the cattle they were expecting. Now *we* were perceived as dangerous to *them*.

"It's funny, in a way. The Seraphim created us to be used according to their will, but in their arrogance they overlooked the history and cultures we've created. A Trojan horse is a specifically human concept—there's no Seraphim equivalent, and so they never saw it coming. And with their immunity already compromised as it was, they had no defense against the virus."

"But what about Alex?"

The old man sighed. "Could I trouble you for one more whiskey?"

The younger man looked conflicted. "You've had a few already. I don't think that's such a good idea."

The old man scowled. "Surely you wouldn't be so cruel to your own grandfather. Especially after learning the hardship of his early life."

The younger man rolled his eyes. "Just so you know, it doesn't count as manipulation if I know I'm being manipulated."

The old man chuckled.

The younger man's fingers danced around the mech-table, and a picture of a cocktail glass, drawn in light, appeared on the table's surface.

"I never get tired of seeing that," the old man said.

"I'll bet."

When the drink was ready, the younger man passed it to his grandfather. "So. Alex?"

The old man smiled. "He died a hero. Naturally. As though these stories could end any other way. No, every story needs a hero, and he was ours."

"I don't understand something," the younger man said.

"And what would that be?"

"How did we get to the way the world is today?"

"What do you mean?"

"With Seraphim and Malakhim living comfortably among us. From your story, it seems like the Seraphim were the enemy to end all enemies, and the alliance with the Malakhim was shaky at best, no?"

"I suppose those things are true, yes."

"So what happened?"

"Time has a way of changing things. It's been almost a century."

The younger man pondered that. "You know what?" he said. "I think I'll have a whiskey myself."

He tapped the instructions into the mech-table, and soon held a glass of the brown liquor himself. He clinked his grandfather's glass.

"How does it feel?" he asked.

"What?" the old man said.

"Knowing your father was the savior of humanity."

The old man's eyes clouded over. "From the way my mother described him, he wouldn't have wanted to be called that, even though that's what he was. I was still months away from being born when he made his great sacrifice, but she made sure I knew the story backward and forward. 'Stories change with time and with who's doing the telling,' Mom used to say. She wanted to make sure I knew, and remembered, how it really happened. From someone who actually lived through it."

"Kate, your mother—"

"And your great-grandmother."

"Went on to have quite a career. A decorated doctor. The surgeon general."

"That's right. She made it her life mission to save lives, and she saved a lot of them. She said she did it to honor my father."

"And she wanted you to keep the story alive?"

"Yes. The way it really happened." He paused, then looked at his grandson. "And now that'll be up to you."

"Well, that's certainly a lot of responsibility."

"Welcome to my world."

The younger man smiled. "We got off topic. You were going to tell me how we got from our apocalyptic relationship with the aliens to the way the world is now."

"Ah, yes. Well, as we said, it's been almost a century since my father Alex gave up his life for us. After he dealt that lethal blow to the Seraphim military, the more gentle-minded of their species sent peace envoys to Earth. The Malakhim, of course, had already helped us immensely with their intelligence and aid. All it took was a few decades for peace talks to get under way, and eventually an alliance formed between all three species."

"Just like that?"

"Well, it was no easy feat, of course. It took a lot of work to build trust. But now we all coexist, even living on each other's planets. There are human beings now who were born on Gan Eden who've never set foot on Earth. Boggles the mind, doesn't it?"

"I guess it does, if you're not used to it," the younger man said. "It's always been a part of my understanding of the universe, though."

"Well, then. Someone did something right."

The younger man took a sip of whiskey and swirled it around in his mouth for a while before swallowing. Something was clearly still on his mind.

"What are you thinking about?" the old man asked.

"Elohim," the younger man said.

"Ah."

"I mean, it's . . . it's a lot."

"Well, the existence of God isn't something that should be simple, now, should it?"

"No. I suppose it shouldn't."

"And, indeed, it isn't."

The younger man took another sip of whiskey. "I guess what confounds me is . . . God is supposed to be unknowable."

"Well, who's to say what's supposed to be and what isn't? But that's how it's always been, yes?"

"For the entirety of human existence."

"Yes."

"I mean, the saints and the insane alike all claimed to speak to God, or that God spoke to them, or what have you, but none of that's ever really been verifiable."

"No."

"But, Grandpa . . . there's still no . . ."

"No what?"

"No evidence. No hard proof."

"But that's always been the thing about faith, hasn't it?" the old man said. "It doesn't come with hard proof."

"But according to your story, the Seraphim . . . they have actual communication with this entity they call Elohim. The one that guided Alex and the rest to Gan Eden . . . what did you say his name was again?"

"Gavreel."

"Gavreel, right. He told Alex he'd spoken with Elohim."

"Yes, that's right."

"But where's the proof of any of this? I mean, if you stop and think about it, what makes the Seraphim any different in their claims than the religious fanatics here on Earth?"

The old man drained his glass of whiskey and set it on the table. He then leaned forward and looked his grandson right in the eye. "Well, now we come to it."

He leaned back and crossed one ancient leg over the other. "As you know, there's been quite a lot of back and forth between Earth and Gan Eden in the subsequent decades since the Harvest War."

The younger man raised his eyebrows. "Yes, I'm aware . . ."

"I have a good friend who's been stationed on Gan Eden for the past nineteen years. A fellow named John Kynlee."

The younger man's eyes widened. "Is he . . ."

"The grandson of Dr. Kynlee, yes. He followed in his grandmother's footsteps and devoted his life to the study of alien biology. He's mostly responsible for all of the direct knowledge we have about the Seraphim's physiology. But he's been doing a lot more than that. In his time there, he's earned the Seraphim's trust like no other human being. And so they decided to do something unprecedented in their history. They've taken an outsider deep within the catacombs of their planet, to a place that John said defied description. The best he could come up with was that it looked like a giant diamond-shaped structure that seemed to be floating in the center of an enormous stone cathedral. Upon a closer look, the majestic tower was actually two separate pyramids. The lower pyramid was inverted, and the base of the upper structure was hovering ever so slightly above the bottom side. The two pyramids were spinning in opposite directions, and each time the corners aligned, a brilliant white light would pulse from deep within. But even that, he said, didn't begin to do it justice."

The younger man's breath caught in his throat. "What were they showing him?"

"John couldn't say, exactly. Except to report that there was . . . something there. Dormant, but present."

The younger man just stared.

"And," the old man said, "earlier today, not one hour before I left my home to come see you, John sent me a message."

He sat there, letting the words hang in the air, until finally the younger man could bear it no longer. "What did the message say?"

The old man leaned forward again, and a smile turned up the corners of his mouth. A smile of hope, and a smile of awe. "Elohim has risen."

The End